T.O.T.J. :

Enjoy Book 5
of the Old Town
mystery series!

Also by John Adam Wasowicz

Daingerfield Island
Jones Point
Slaters Lane
Roaches Run

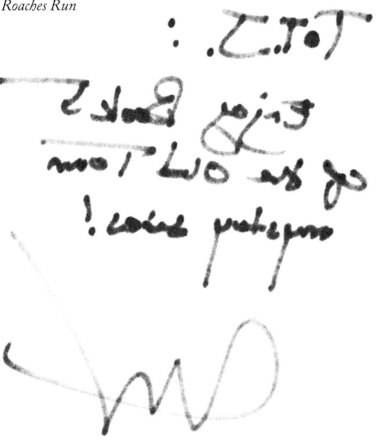

GADSBY'S CORNER

John Adam Wasowicz

"Poirot," I said. "I have been thinking."
"An admirable exercise my friend. Continue it."

— Agatha Christie, *Peril at End House*

GADSBY'S CORNER

Publisher: John Adam Wasowicz
Editor: Charles Rammelkamp
Graphic Design: Ace Kieffer
Cover art: Alex Herron Wasowicz
Author photo: Robin T. Herron

Alendron Publishing LLC 2022
3005 Wessynton Way
Alexandria, VA 22309

Distributor: Itasca Books, Inc.

ISBN: 979-8-9858307-3-6

Printed in the United States of America

To Clarinda Harriss, with gratitude

TABLE OF CONTENTS

Part One
7:00 to 9:00 p.m.

Chapter One — *Murder in the Museum*.................................15

Chapter Two — The Five Ws.................................19

Chapter Three — TJK.................................23

Chapter Four — Quinn Who?.................................28

Chapter Five — My Mai.................................31

Chapter Six — The Madding Crowd.................................35

Chapter Seven — Squeeze Play.................................42

Chapter Eight — Dang.................................47

Chapter Nine — Here Comes My Man.................................50

Chapter Ten — *Pardonnez-Moi*.................................57

Chapter Eleven — Mari, Maddie, Marnie, Mimi.................................59

Chapter Twelve — The Z That Stands for Zara.................................66

Chapter Thirteen — Mixing Irish Coffee with a Martini.................................70

Chapter Fourteen — Kiss Me, You Fool.................................73

Chapter Fifteen — Rows and Mews.................................77

Chapter Sixteen — This Heart of Stone.................................82

Chapter Seventeen — Drinks and Drabs.................................85

Part Two
9:00 to 11:00 p.m.

Chapter Eighteen — *Rhythmic Circles*.................................93

Chapter Nineteen — *Murder in the Museum*.................................97

Chapter Twenty — Mo than Meets the Eye.................................101

Chapter Twenty-one — The Dirty Dozen..........................106

Chapter Twenty-two — The Murder Room......................111

Chapter Twenty-three — The 2 Ms..................................113

Chapter Twenty-four — Teller Me the Truth...................121

Chapter Twenty-five — It's All the Rage..........................125

Chapter Twenty-six — I Feel Sorry for You.....................129

Chapter Twenty-seven — Deng It....................................133

Chapter Twenty-eight — Up on the Roof........................138

Chapter Twenty-nine — ZZ Bottom................................141

Chapter Thirty — A Silver Sliver.....................................144

Chapter Thirty-one — Calling Around...........................148

Chapter Thirty-two — Luis Luis.....................................153

Chapter Thirty-three — Operator, Smooth Operator.....157

Chapter Thirty-four — Head Out on the Highway.........161

Part Three
After 11:00 p.m.

Chapter Thirty-five — One More for the Road................165

Chapter Thirty-six — Padington Station.........................167

Chapter Thirty-seven — Goin' Down, Down, Down........172

Chapter Thirty-eight — Point of Clarification................178

Chapter Thirty-nine — Teller Me More...........................187

Chapter Forty — Charles on the Stand...........................189

Chapter Forty-one — Glasses of a Different Sort............198

Chapter Forty-two — Riddle Me Charles........................202

Chapter Forty-three — My Cousin Michael....................207

Chapter Forty-four — The Iceman Cometh.....................211

Chapter Forty-five — The Murderer Is Revealed.............215

Chapter Forty-six — Three to Get Ready............................216

Chapter Forty-seven — And in the End...............................224

Chapter Forty-eight — The Spirits of Old Town.......................228

Chapter Forty-nine — Everybody's Got Something to Hide......230

Chapter Fifty — Home Sweet Home...................................234

Part One
7:00 to 9:00 p.m.

Chapter One — *Murder in the Museum*

"David Reese!" A voice called across the hall.

I had just opened the door to Gadsby's Tavern Museum and stuffed my dripping umbrella into a stand already crammed with large beach umbrellas, green-and-white-striped golf umbrellas, umbrellas with broken ribs, plastic bags, drenched newspapers, towels, you name it. People had obviously grabbed anything within reach before making a mad dash from their cars to the museum. I shook off my sopping jacket and handed it to the coat checker.

It was dreadful outside. Sheets of rain were falling on Old Town and throughout the Washington, D.C., area. Lower King Street was going to be submerged once again, just like it always is when there's a torrential downpour.

If this monsoon had been forecast, I doubt anyone would be here tonight. But this storm sneaked up without warning. Hopefully it will dissipate by the time the evening's performance is over.

A few years ago, a flash flood would have been a newsworthy event. Not anymore. A friend of mine nearly drowned along the George Washington Parkway under the 14th Street Bridge during an unexpected downpour just the other week. She had to climb through the roof of her BMW and swim to safety. On the parkway, mind you!

According to news reports, 85 percent of the world's population has experienced some form of extreme climate event. Tonight seems to be our turn. To keep up with the extreme weather, I've learned new weather words, like derecho [deh-REY-cho], which is defined as a hurricane-tornado combo.

Fortunately, it's nice and dry inside the museum. The place is packed. The hallway, the meeting room, and the staircase are all filled with people. Loud voices and hearty laughter fill the air. *Everyone* is here, which is surprising for an amateur production of *Murder in the Museum*.

I suspect it had something to do with our need to reacquaint ourselves with one another following the pandemic.

I mean there's only so much you can take. First Covid-19, then the Delta variant, followed by Omicron. It took me a while to learn how to pronounce that word: omicron. It's a pretty menacing name, don't you think?

I may be one of the few people who isn't here to mingle. I'm not even interested in the production. I got a ticket to *Murder in the Museum* for a specific purpose. I want to reconcile with Mai Lin, my wife. I know she's going to be here with U.S. Attorney Mo Katz and his entourage. I'm looking for a convenient opportunity to run into her. Hopefully, it will appear coincidental.

"David! David Reese, over here," the voice bellowed.

I spotted Professor Michael Charles, my old torts professor. Only his hands and head were visible. He's probably 5 foot 6, and that's being generous. His hands, which are raised and flapping at me, stick out in a sea of heads and shoulders. Every once in a while, the dome of his head appears, like a balloon: a huge bald globe surrounded by a wisp of hair that resembles Caesar's laurels, only white instead of gold.

As I watch Charles navigate through crowd, elbowing his way toward me, I'm reminded how long it's been since I attended any indoor public event. With the exception of work at the Commonwealth Attorney's Office in Old Town, I've basically confined myself to home since March 2020.

Okay, I attended the Snallygaster Beer Festival last October, but that was an outdoor event so it doesn't really count.

The social scene is reawakening throughout Northern Virginia. Mount Vernon is open, as is the Lyceum, Carlyle House, and the Stabler-Leadbeater Apothecary Museum. I think the Lee-Fendall House is conducting tours by appointment. I'm not sure about the Black History Museum or Freedom House. I'll check their schedules online when I get home.

This event was initially scheduled for last fall but it got pushed back due to COVID-19. Better safe than sorry. Actually, the timing appears to have worked to my advantage. This is a perfect venue to try to reconcile with Mai.

"David, so nice to see you," said Charles, coming alongside me.

"I didn't know you were a fan of Henry David McLuhan," I said, giving him a quick once-over. Same old Michael Charles, always dresses the same: blue blazer, wrinkled khakis, and topsiders, which are actually appropriate for tonight's weather.

"Who?" His face belied any knowledge of tonight's festivities. He pushed his glasses up on the bridge of his nose with his right index finger.

"You're not here for *Murder in the Museum*, are you?" I asked.

It sounded accusatory, but I didn't mean it that way. It comes from examining too many witnesses in trials, I guess. I'm an assistant commonwealth attorney. I've just been promoted to senior assistant, which is a pretty big deal since I've only been on the job a couple of years. Nobody has racked up more convictions in less time than me.

"I was supposed to be on the twilight garden tour," he explains. "I've never been here before. I don't know anything about this place. They stuffed us inside here when our tour was cancelled. It was clear at dusk, nary a cloud in the sky. What happened?"

Well, that explained it. The overcrowded building wasn't due to people dying to see Henry David McLuhan or thirsting to get out of the house and resume gathering in public places. This was simply an odd confluence of circumstances caused by a turn in the weather. It certainly didn't seem to be the sort of get-together that would result in a murder, although that's what's going to happen in two and a half hours, give or take a few minutes.

By the way, I just finished prosecuting a murder, which is a rarity in Old Town, I'm happy to say. There may be a spike in violent crime in most of our nation's major cities, but serious crime is pretty rare around here.

In case you're wondering, the defendant in that case got a life sentence. It's one of the fifteen felony convictions I've sustained. When defense attorneys see me coming, they run or encourage their clients to plead out. I'm not bragging, I'm just stating the facts. And juries love me.

Literally.

I had a brief affair with a juror. But, before you start casting aspersions, you should know that the case was over, the verdict was in, and the jury had been discharged. And she contacted me. She initiated it! What was I supposed to do, consult ethics counsel before succumbing to her entreaties? Sorry, I'm not trying to sound sarcastic.

Anyway, she was infatuated with me. Who could blame her? I seduce juries. She said I was mesmerizing. Her words. Between us, she wasn't exaggerating.

I never told Mai about that indiscretion, which makes me a bit of a cad. Still, since she doesn't know about that one, I think it actually increases the odds of her forgiving me for my current indiscretion. While I'm not going into details, this one has been taken totally out of context.

Sigh! I know I have to do better. I'm trying.

But listen, enough about me.

Chapter Two — The Five Ws

Before we go further, let's do the whole who, what, when, where, and why of the story.

The five Ws. These are the basic tenets of any piece of journalism, which I know from taking a class in high school. Though I have to say, I find them absent from most pieces of modern journalism. Today, everyone editorializes about everything. To the extent they write a "hard news" story — which is rare — it's still tilted either to the right or to the left.

It used to be that you could find the truth on the front page of the newspaper. Then you had to read both the left-leaning and the right-leaning publications to glean the truth. It took time, but you could do it. Now, however, everyone is so tribal and everything is so polarized it's hard to figure out if there's any truth to be had at all.

Fortunately, you aren't going to find any spin with me. No slanting, no taking sides, no attempt to falsify information or mislead you. I'm simply writing a good, old-fashioned mystery. Actually, it's a retelling, but I'll get to that in a minute.

Let's go over the basics:

Who. I'm David Reese. I'm 31 years old. I'm married to Mai Lin. We have a son, born in 2019.

I'm from Milwaukee, Wisconsin. I have an undergraduate degree in psychology from George Washington University and a law degree from Georgetown. As I've already told you a couple of times, I'm a prosecutor in the City of Alexandria.

My parents divorced a few years ago, which I think is weird because I was raised in a loving home and I don't know what possessed them to end their marriage. My father lives alone on a houseboat in Sarasota, Florida. My mom moved back to Saratoga, New York, to take care of her parents, who are elderly. I used to love visiting there in August and going to the track.

I know it's strange: one parent moves to Sarasota and the other to Saratoga. What are the chances of that?

Mai Lin is the love of my life. She keeps me grounded and I enjoy her company more than anyone else's in the world, with the possible exception of our son. She's a brilliant researcher for Mo Katz, the U.S. attorney for the Eastern District of Virginia. We met at GW. She has a degree in forensics.

Our family lives in Fairlington in a two-bedroom condo on the third floor of a brick and slate-roofed building. The unit has a spiral staircase and a loft over the dining/living room area. It has a small kitchen and one bathroom. It's lovely.

Well, I should qualify that statement. I'm currently crashing at a friend's parents' home. I hope to soon move back to Fairlington. We'll see how it goes.

What. I'm attending *Murder in the Museum*, a fundraiser put together by the Gadsby's Tavern Museum Society, a nonprofit that supports the work of the museum.

Murder in the Museum is supposed to be one of those "Clue"-like mysteries that follows an Agatha Christie formula where there is a murder and a long list of potential suspects. The event is supposed to begin around 8 p.m. and will be moderated — if that's the right word — by Henry David McLuhan, the author and self-help guru.

Mo Katz and some members of his entourage — including Mai and Curtis Santana, Mo's chief investigator in the U.S. Attorney's Office — wrote the script. I've got a copy of it in my pocket. Mo is supposed to participate in it, along with some local personalities.

The event was originally scheduled for October 22, 2021, but was postponed because of the pandemic. At that time, the program included Classical WETA's Nicole Lacroix; Arlington icon Bill Newman; radio and television personality Derek McGinty; narrator Jim Cuddy; Ralph Peluso, the literary critic of Alexandria's Zebra Press; and Ciera Shine, who does a weekly program on WPFW, a District radio station.

The cast got reconfigured for tonight's event.

Ironically, there will be a real murder tonight. I'm not prescient when I say that to you. I'm just recapping events. When the murder occurred, banner headlines were splashed across the front pages of the local newspapers. It was the lead story on Channels 4, 5, 7 and 9 for about three days running.

Except none of the news reports told the whole story. That's why I've chosen to write about it. To create a sense of immediacy, I've written a first-person account in the present tense. I'm being honest, though, and telling you that I keep slipping into the past tense. I don't know if you've ever tried it, but writing isn't easy, particularly when it comes to keeping tenses in order. If I mess up, I hope you'll cut me some slack and just write it off. No pun intended.

The script for *Murder in the Museum* in my pocket is highlighted for clues. Like this: CLUE. I co-opted that technique to let you know when you should be paying attention to this story.

When. It happened on a Friday night in the spring of 2022 during a monsoon that practically drowned the entire city. You wouldn't believe the damage it caused throughout the city, especially down by the waterfront at the base of King Street, which always floods in a storm. You know, they really should do something about that.

Where. The venue is Gadsby's Tavern Museum, a large colonial brick building located on the corner of Royal and Cameron Streets in the middle of Old Town, a block from City Hall. It's actually two buildings with a tavern on the first floor of one of them. Rather than describe the museum to you, just go to the website. Here's the link: https://www.alexandriava.gov/GadsbysTavern.

I'd never visited the museum or the tavern before the night of the murder. After you read this account, I hope you'll drop by and retrace my steps.

Why. I'm not sure I understand the question. Why was there a murder? Well, I'm not going to tell you that, at least not now. It'd spoil the fun.

If, however, the question is, "Why are you writing about it?" I'll be candid and tell you I'm a little jealous that Mo Katz gets so much publicity for his exploits. A series of books chronicles his exploits, including *Daingerfield Island, Jones Point, Slaters Lane,* and *Roaches Run.* He's become somewhat of a Sherlock Holmes-type figure in Old Town, which is highly unusual given the fact that he's the U.S. attorney for the Eastern District of Virginia.

The letter "i" appears twice in Daingerfield. That's not a typo. John Daingerfield was a big property owner in Alexandria back in the day. There's also a street named after him, around the corner from Harvard Street, where Mo Katz lives with his girlfriend, Abby Snowe. They're foster parents for a little girl, Katie Fortune, whose parents are dead.

I'd like to be recognized for my contributions. After all, I was involved in the cases depicted in the books. For example, it was I who found the photo from the locket worn by the victim whose body was pulled from the Potomac River off Daingerfield Island.

I'm not trying to hog the spotlight, I'm honestly not, but I am trying to make a point: Solving murders is a team sport. There is no "I" in murder. The only way to get some of the glory, if I can be so bold, is to seize the narrative. Otherwise, I'm just another character in the story.

Got it?

Chapter Three — TJK

"What are you drinking?" Charles asked. I noticed that he held a long-stemmed glass with a large delicate bowl, sort of like a fishbowl on a spike, filled with red wine.

"What have they got?" I asked.

"Everything," he replied. His glasses slipped down his oily nose. He pushed them up with his index finger again.

"Then why are you drinking wine?" I asked.

He frowned.

"I'm serious," I said. "If they have everything here — whiskey, bourbon, gin, vodka, liqueurs — why did you settle for a glass of red wine? That's boring."

"Actually, I don't drink," he said. "This is a prop. I'll have it in my hand all night long but I'll never raise it to my lips. It's like a security blanket. It gives me something to do with my hands."

Now I remembered. He was once a bad drunk. In fact, he nearly got thrown off the faculty. He used to come to class intoxicated, if you can believe it. He would have been tossed out years ago but for the fact that he's popular, brilliant, and comes from a wealthy New England family that has contributed mightily to the law school.

"I might not either," I said. "Drink, that is." I didn't mean it, of course. I was atoning for having recited all those alcoholic beverages to him. It might have been enough to nearly throw him off the wagon, which was not my intention.

Suddenly, I noticed a despondent look on his face. Was he sick? "What's wrong?" I asked.

"I've been trying to…" His eyes welled with tears. He closed his eyes, trying to douse the tears. It didn't help. The tears seeped out and rolled down his cheeks.

He lowered his head, cupped his hand over his face, and pressed his thumb and middle finger over his closed eyelids as though he was squeezing a lemon. Then he raised his head, opened his eyes, took a deep breath, and started to say something about his dog. I didn't know he had a dog, which just goes to show you might know less about a person than you think you do.

My attention was suddenly diverted as Theodosia Jaidah Kessler entered the large meeting room, referred to as the Grand Room. The marvelous TJK. Nobody calls her by her full name. She's too well known, plus her middle name is hard to remember and pronounce. It's sort of like Alexandria Ocasio-Cortez. So much easier to have a name that's easily recognized as an acronym. It's not the least bit insulting; it actually conveys fame and familiarity, like FDR or JFK.

As much as I liked Michael Charles and as curious as I was to know more about the source of his despondency, my eyes and mind shifted focus. They were aimed exclusively on TJK, the goddess of Old Town Alexandria.

Tall and statuesque, with black hair pulled to the side and cascading over her right shoulder like a waterfall, TJK didn't simply walk into a room. She swept into it. Thin loop earrings dangled daintily from her ears. A magnificent bronze necklace adorned her neck and touched the top of her ample cleavage. Her brown eyes shone like polished gems. Her skin was as smooth as marble and her smile as beguiling as da Vinci's Mona Lisa. To top it off, her full lips were painted a deep red.

Staring at her was like looking into the sun during an eclipse. I averted my eyes for fear my pupils would incur permanent damage.

A few months ago, TJK accompanied a witness to my office on an assault and battery case. She provided moral support to the victim. I'm sure she remembers me. She certainly seemed appreciative of the assistance I rendered to her friend.

My mind wandered as I recalled the case. The victim was a Miss Virginia beauty contestant. She alleged physical abuse at the hand of Ronnie Coates, a well-known Alexandria entrepreneur.

Entrepreneur is a fancy word for a jack of all trades whose claim to wealth is both mysterious and mercurial. Many people referred to

Jeffrey Epstein as an entrepreneur. While I don't put Coates in the same category as Epstein — there is no suggestion that Coates was ever involved in trafficking underage girls for sex — I do assign the same ambiguity as to his professional credentials.

Plus, the details of the physical abuse that the beauty queen alleged were reprehensible. I'm not going to go into details. Suffice it to say it was nasty stuff. Upon learning of Coates' misdeeds, TJK wrapped her loving arm around the beauty queen, accompanied her to the Commonwealth Attorney's Office, and demanded that we do something about it.

I took the victim's statement. Misdemeanor warrants were issued. The police arrested Coates. I argued for a high bail and demanded a temporary restraining order to ensure the woman's protection. The judge granted both requests. At arraignment, Coates pled not guilty and we set the case down for trial.

As a plea bargain, I offered six months in jail on each of three counts to be run concurrently. Coates and his attorney laughed in my face, as I expected and secretly hoped would be the case. I wanted to bait them.

"Drop two counts and we'll plead straight up," Coates' attorney countered. Coates and the attorney gambled that the judge would never put him in jail and, if she did so, it would never be for six months. I saw it differently and figured I had nothing to lose.

A&B is a class one misdemeanor carrying a maximum penalty of a year in jail. Whether I got one or three convictions was of little significance when you figure I wanted six months as the plea bargain. The key was to put him behind bars as a penalty for his transgression.

I warned Coates' attorney that he was making a mistake. "If you've miscalculated, your client could end up in jail for a year," I said. Once again, I didn't do it to help Coates. I wanted him to dismiss my warning. The haughtier the better, I say.

"We'll take our chances," said the attorney, which was code for

"F off."

"We shall see," said I.

The plea was tendered. The sentencing hearing took place about two weeks ago. Neither Coates nor his counsel knew that the district court judge was herself a victim of domestic violence. Of course, being the recipient of courtroom gossip, I knew it. So did TJK, as it turned out, which surprised me because it was one of those things that is usually confined to the courthouse crowd. Since Coates' attorney hailed from neighboring Loudoun County, he wasn't privy to any insider information.

"Does the judge have an obligation to inform the other side?" TJK asked me before the sentencing. I appreciated her desire to see that everyone comported to the appropriate ethical rules.

"Not sure," I answered, "but I don't think so. There's no public record about any domestic violence case involving the judge." The clerks had checked, if you're wondering how I knew. "It's all gossip and innuendo. If the judge feels she can't be objective, it would be her responsibility to remove herself."

I'll grant you that it was an obtuse response, but it satisfied TJK. "Good," TJK replied. "She's going to nail his ass."

At the sentencing, I called the beauty queen to the stand. She testified about the physical and psychological scars that had been inflicted upon her. Everyone in the courtroom teared up. Next, I presented evidence from her therapist, who confirmed the long-term trauma that originated from the abuse.

By the time the sentencing hearing was over, some people were probably wondering why I hadn't pursued felony charges. I was wondering about it myself, to be honest.

The judge handed down a twelve-month sentence.

And then....

Oh, my gosh!

Michael Charles has been talking all the while I have been in my reverie, going on and on about his dog. His head is bowed. And he's bawling.

He looked up at me, red-faced and teary-eyed, expecting me to reply to his bearing his soul.

Chapter Four — Quinn Who?

I must confess I hardly heard a word. A snippet here and a snippet there, at best. "…the limo driver…" and "…she didn't so much as express any sorrow…." and "…an absolute abomination…" and "Quinn."

I handed him a napkin I'd picked up from a food tray nearby. He blew his nose into it and tried to hand the napkin back to me. I didn't take it. He wrapped it around his wine glass stem. I noticed that, true to his word, he hadn't taken a sip of wine, which still sloshed around in that fishbowl-sized globe.

My lack of focus was apparent.

"You haven't heard a thing I said, did you?" he asked accusingly. "You've been daydreaming about her, haven't you?" He cocked his head disgustedly in the direction of TJK.

"That's not true," I lied. "I heard every word. You poor man. To have lost such a loyal companion. What a terrible loss," I said.

It was a total guess. Even if I hadn't heard a word of his incessant babbling, I could deduce the dog was dead. I could play empathetic. It worked.

He removed his glasses, dabbed his eyes with the wet, snotty napkin, and blew his nose again. "Thank you for listening," he said. He replaced the glasses, which immediately slid down the bridge of his nose.

"You know she's not all sweetness and light," he said, lowering his voice. He was now looking over at TJK. I inferred he'd said something about her a moment ago, but I hadn't picked up on it. "It might surprise you to know it's how she manages to remain flush with cash." I was totally lost. Before I could inquire, he muttered indistinguishably. I strained. *Backgammon? Back Bay?* What did he say?

Before I could ask him to repeat the utterance, he reached into the pocket of his blazer and removed a rolled-up dog leash. It was a short leash, not one of those leashes on a spring spool that you can control like a tape measure.

"It's Quinn's leash," he said.

Quinn? That's the name of his dog? Who names their dog Quinn?

Bob Dylan once wrote a song titled "Quinn the Eskimo (The Mighty Quinn)" that was a Top 40 hit with the title "The Mighty Quinn" by Manfred Mann. It was an okay song, but not great. My favorite Dylan cover is "All Along the Watchtower" performed by Jimi Hendrix. The guitar riff in that song gives me goosebumps every time I hear it.

The fact that Michael Charles is carrying Quinn's leash in his pocket suggested he'd lost the dog recently, possibly earlier in the day. All that remained of the dog was his leash, the personal effects of the deceased. I regretted I'd been distracted and focused upon TJK instead of listening to Charles' story.

"That's such a compelling story," I said, hoping to spur him to repeat something. Anything.

"It's so sad," he acknowledged. "I really don't want to bore you, but I could talk about it all night."

"If it helps you to grieve, I'm here to listen," I said.

All I got at this point was an abridged version, but it was better than nothing. I gathered that some reckless driver had hit the dog earlier this morning.

"If the facility had remained open, Quinn could have gotten emergency treatment," he said. "But of course it was already boarded up and ready to be torn down. In a strange way, I feel as though the dog gods punished me. I played a role in directing the wrecking ball to the building. If I had not done that, Quinn might be alive tonight."

He swished the wine around in the fishbowl. For a second, I thought he was going to take a swig.

"Thanks for sharing," I said. I muttered some other inane words of consolation. But I'm thinking, *The dog gods! The man had totally lost it.*

"Thanks for listening," he said.

"Say, let's take a photo together," I said. I took out my phone and clicked to the camera setting. He turned. I put my arm around him. He held out his wine glass as though he was toasting me. I snapped the photo. "It looks great," I said. "What's your email address? I'll send you a copy."

He provided the address to me. I emailed him a copy. He expressed his gratitude.

Having saved face with Michael Charles, I turned and beat a speedy retreat, leaving him standing forlornly in the middle of an ever-increasing crowd with a soggy napkin, a dog leash, and an untouched glass of red wine. Within seconds, the little man was obscured in a forest of much taller men and women.

I went in search of TJK.

Chapter Five — My Mai

Where was she? Whereas Michael Charles vanished among taller people, TJK was not one to get lost in a crowd. Seas parted for her.

Apparently, that wasn't the case tonight. I looked down the hall and around corners. I ascended the staircases and searched the upstairs rooms. She was nowhere to be seen. Where was she? Where had she vanished?

As I asked these questions, I went back downstairs and surveyed the Grand Room.

"There may be a black sky outside, but the stars are here at Gadsby's Tavern Museum," I heard someone say.

I agreed. It was a star-studded V.I.P. list. And I was part of it. I know most of the movers and shakers in this city. And, at the risk of sounding pretentious, they know me. It's the truth.

There's Mari Teller, holding a snifter filled with brandy. She's got something to do with planning and development in the city. It's some volunteer position on some community service board. To listen to her, you'd think she was the city manager, which she most certainly is not, though she apparently carries some weight in political circles if for no reason other than her longevity.

It seems as though she's been on the commission since Virginia declared its independence from Great Britain, or at least since Virginia seceded from the Union. Fickle state, when you think about it. Maybe that's why Virginia is a classic purple state; it's always shifting from blue to red and then back again. Hard to predict, just like some of the people in this room.

Before I forget, there are going to be a lot of digressions in this story, so you might as well get used to it. If that bothers or offends you, close the book now. I have the attention span of a goldfish. I go from one thing to another without the slightest provocation or care. Like when I was half listening to Michael Charles while thinking about TJK and the Coates trial. I'm all over the place. Always have been, always will be. I guess I was just born this way.

I love that line: "Born This Way." It's the title of a song by Lady Gaga written by her and Jeppe Laursen. Although it's over ten years old, that song is still popular, and the title has been appropriated in myriad ways, like the slogan "Born This Gay."

Why is it so popular? I'll tell you. It's simple, direct, and true.

Simple. Direct. True. Those words best describe my aspiration whenever I am doing trial work. Keep it simple. Be direct. And, for goodness' sake, tell the truth or get off the stage. Even if you can't remember all ten of the Commandments, or even if you can remember them but can't abide by all of them all of the time, keep those three traits in mind in whatever you think, say, or do and you'll be okay.

I'm so absorbed in myself right now that I didn't notice I was walking smack dab into my wife, Mai.

"Hey, Mai, how are you?" I asked.

"David, why are you here?" she asked in surprise.

Her tone was extremely cold and even a little accusatory, as though I wasn't supposed to be there in the first place. It's not like I just appeared magically in her bedroom or anything. Correction: *our* bedroom.

Of course, I don't actually have keys to our condo at the present time. I voluntarily gave them to Mai to give her some space. Actually, that's not entirely true. I acted under some duress because there was a possibility she would change the locks if I didn't give the keys to her.

Ours is not necessarily an amicable separation, but she hasn't sought an injunction or keep away order and she hasn't filed for divorce. So I'm hopeful we can work things out. I'm just waiting for the right moment.

In the best of times, Mai and I are a team, like Rodgers and Hart, Abbott and Costello, Jagger and Richards. Give us the right ingredients and we can cook up the most spectacular stuff. Who knows, maybe we'll have a chance to do something together tonight. Spoiler alert: We do. And it revolves around murder.

But I'm getting ahead of myself. Let me go back to my separation from Mai. In the final analysis, it's a problem of communication. That's always the case. People don't talk to one another, you know. It's not a new phenomenon. It's why couples separate, neighbors fight, and nations go to war. So many bad things could be avoided if people simply talked things out.

Okay, that and my infidelity, or alleged infidelity, however you want to put it.

"Seriously, why are you here?" she repeated.

"I wanted to catch *Murder in the Museum*," I answered. "I heard Mo was putting on the skit and that you and the crew were helping out. I thought I'd drop by and say 'hi' to the whole gang."

Gosh, that sounded so phony. And it appeared she was buying it. How could I do this, particularly after just commenting about the importance of communication and expounding on the virtues of simplicity, directness, and truth?

"Actually, that's not true," I said. "I came here specifically to run into you. I wanted it to appear coincidental and casual and everything, but the fact is it's deliberate on my part. I don't care about the *Murder* thing. I wanted to see you. I want to reconcile. I want to come home."

She looked deep into my eyes the way Larry David does in *Curb My Enthusiasm*.

"What did you say?" she asked.

I tried very hard to assess the situation before I answered. She meant one of two things. Either she concluded that I'm stalking her and that she really should get a restraining order or she's impressed with my candor and honesty.

"I came here to run into you," I said, going for the latter. "I was going to pretend it was coincidental, but it's not. I wanted to find a moment to talk to you. I want to apologize. I want us to get back together."

Just then Curtis Santana appeared. "Hey, David," he said coldly. Curtis is a friend of mine but a closer confidant of Mai's. Therefore, he probably thinks I'm a total shit. He then looked directly at her, ignoring me. "Are you ready?" he asked. "Mo wants to do a dry run. Plus, Henry David is here. We need to set up and run through the script."

Turning to me, she said blandly, "We'll talk later." With that, she departed.

I was left clueless as to which way she was leaning, which is a shame. I might have been making an inroad. Or maybe I'm really still out in the cold. It would be good to know which way she's leaning. If I have my way, I won't be returning tonight to my friend's parents' basement.

As she and Santana retreated, I noticed Henry David McLuhan. The man is a piece of work, trust me.

To begin with, Henry David McLuhan is his nom de plume, a composite of Henry David Thoreau and Marshall McLuhan. Some people might think that's cool, but I think it's pretentious. His real name is Ari Hammond.

Last year, McLuhan (or Hammond, take your pick) was mixed up with Mo Katz in the Roaches Run case. I'm not sure exactly how it went down, but I think Katz deduced that McLuhan was involved in a bombing and death. Katz doesn't talk about it. All I know is one day McLuhan was a suspect in a murder and the next day he was flying to Paris. It's all very suspicious.

McLuhan is the author of *The Rhythmic Cycle of Life*, a self-help book based on the theory that life repeats itself in twelve-year cycles. If you can figure out the high points and low points of your cycle, you can avoid calamities on the next go-around and lean into opportunities, or at least that's the theory. Again, highly suspicious and pretentious.

Chapter Six — The Madding Crowd

The Grand Room was SRO. Boisterous conversation and shrieks of laughter punctuated the atmosphere and created a cacophony of rich sound. I don't know about you, but I love the sound of a crowd. I always have. Since the lockdown during the pandemic, I enjoy it more than ever. At least I think I do.

During the pandemic, silence permeated our lives. Things that we took for granted vanished, including the chatter of a crowd, the clicking of glasses, the clatter of dishes, and the entire orchestral sound that accompanies an assemblage. Silence is okay, but it has its place, like at Walden Pond.

I'm still thinking about TJK. I can't find her anywhere. Of course, given the size of the crowd, that's hardly surprising. Since I'm unable to locate her, let's see who else is here.

There's a distinguished threesome engaged in conversation: Luis Aquila, a state delegate from Fairfax, rumored to be making a run for lieutenant governor in 2025; Katlin Ash Brook, a real estate magnate; and philanthropist Siri Deng, who is deeply invested in rDNA vaccine development or something of that nature.

Near them stands retired journalist-turned-author Bernie Hill, who just published a tell-all about the Reagan administration. I purchased a copy. It's remarkable how far we've fallen down the political ladder since the '80s, and that's all the more remarkable when you consider the political dissension that existed at that time.

According to the history books, we were filled with optimism 40 years ago. Ronald Reagan called us the beacon of hope for the world. "America is a shining city upon a hill whose beacon light guides freedom-loving people everywhere," he said. I read it in Hill's book.

We were suddenly the world's only superpower. The Berlin Wall was coming down. We envisioned a world in which peace might extend across Europe and then around the globe. Now look at things! There's destruction and desolation as far as the eye can see as Putin's troops cross into Ukraine. So much for utopian visions.

Did you know that TJK was the youngest ambassador in the Reagan administration? I think she was ambassador to India. Maybe it was Mauritius. I'm not sure. Does the U.S. have an ambassador to Mauritius?

Hill is engaged in conversation with socialite Monica Livingston.

Bernie Hill is an old, frumpy, matronly-looking man. Something about his cheekbones and red lips, both of which create the image that he's wearing makeup. His face is like Robin Williams' Mrs. Doubtfire.

Hill seems harmless enough, but you know what they say about that type. They're the axe murderers and arsonists hiding innocently among us. Remember: For every cold case, there's a red-hot murderer running around somewhere. Bernie Hill fits the mold.

Hill came to Washington from New Orleans.

Everyone in Washington, by the way, comes from somewhere else. It used to be that, whenever the Washington Nationals played, the "fans" in the ballpark rooted for their home team, which was invariably the opposition. Whenever the Red Sox or Brewers visited, the place was full of people from Boston or Milwaukee. That phenomenon ceased during the spectacular 2019 World Series run, but it's already coming back, especially since all of the people who gave us that magical year have been traded.

It's less true for the Washington Commanders or the Caps. I'm not sure why. Maybe there are just more football and hockey fans in D.C. who are loyal to the home team. And, speaking of the Commanders, I can't help but think that sports editors are glad they don't have to worry about mixing up the letters in the previous acronym, WFT. I mean, imagine this possible headline: "WTF: Playoffs Are a Possibility."

Hill's New Orleans roots are on prominent display from the

glass he's holding in his hand. His cocktail of choice, you see, is a Hurricane, a mixture of rum, lemon juice, and either fassionola or passion fruit syrup. It's a mainstay in the Big Easy. A dead giveaway for the drink is that it's served in a tall and curvy eponymous hurricane glass.

If you don't know, eponymous means the glassware bears the same name as the drink itself. This also applies to an old fashioned or a martini. It would not apply to, say a Dark 'n Stormy, which is my favorite drink.

Now that I think of it, though, it would be cool if there was unique glassware for a Dark 'n Stormy, which, for the uninitiated, is a combination of dark rum and ginger beer served over ice. I prefer mine with a slice of lime in lieu of lime juice or syrup. If that sounds to you like a Moscow mule, it is, except that the mule has vodka instead of dark rum.

One more thing while we're on the subject of dark and stormy. Those words are included in one of the oft stated literary lines of all time, right up there with "It was the best of times, it was the worst of times" and "Hell hath no fury like a woman scorned."

Here's the entire sentence:

It was a dark and stormy night; the rain fell in torrents — except at occasional intervals, when it was checked by a violent gust of wind which swept up the streets, rattling along the housetops, and fiercely agitating the scanty flame of the lamps that struggled against the darkness.

Those lines could easily describe tonight's scene. Mai and I used to utter them incessantly when we went on evening strolls. (Gosh, I miss those walks.) Here's the question: Who wrote that line? I'll give you three choices: (a) Charles Dickens, whose reference to "the best of times" is the opening line of his classic *A Tale of Two Cities*; (b) Edgar Allen Poe, the master of the macabre; or (c) Edward Bulwer-Lytton.

If you guessed (c), you're correct. Surprised? I mean, everyone selects (b). But it turns out that "dark and stormy" is the opening line of Bulwer-Lytton's 1830 novel, *Paul Clifford*. I know. Who's Edward Bulwer-Lytton, right? I have no idea. And who ever read the book? Better yet, who ever heard of the book? Nobody, probably, except people like me searching for the origin of the famous phrase. Be that as it may, I'm sure it's a delightfully entertaining piece of literature.

Anyway, I managed to get a Dark 'n Stormy before I saw Hill and Livingston engaged in conversation. This drink is delicious, by the way. Back to them. Enough about Hill. Let's talk about Livingston.

People always confuse Monica Livingston with Monica Lewinsky. It's the name.

"Monica Lewinsky is here? Where? Oh, that doesn't look anything like Monica Lewinsky!" I hear that all the time.

There's actually no comparison. Livingston is a Hollywood transplant who's rumored to be close to Prince Harry and Meghan, the Duke and Duchess of Sussex. She's reportedly helping them film a fictional account of an affair between the British prime minister and the U.S. president. It's not a gay story, though that would be tantalizing. The prime minister is reportedly modeled after Margaret Thatcher. The '80s are in vogue, I guess.

Livingston probably roots for the Dodgers whenever she goes to Nats Park, assuming she goes at all, because she doesn't strike me as much of a baseball fan, or sport in general, unless it's a women's sports team.

While we're talking about Washington's sports teams, how many people know that the Washington Mystics were the other team that won a championship in 2019? Probably only a few more than know that the Washington Spirit won the NWSL championship last year.

What? You knew about both the Mystics and Spirit championships? Really? Well, not that I doubt you, but I'm skeptical by nature so let me test your sports acumen. Name three members on the Mystics roster.

Just like I thought.

I can name three off the top of my head: Ariel Atkins and two-time MVP Elena Delle Donne. Okay, that's only two, but it's still better than what you've got. And, while I'm at it, here are the names of some of the stars on the Spirits roster: Andi Sullivan, Tara McKeown, and Ashley Hatch.

Wait a minute.

I remember the names of a few more players on the Mystics roster: Natasha Cloud, Megan Gustafson, and Myisha Hines-Allen. If you're impressed, don't be. I put down my Dark 'n Stormy, pulled out my phone, and looked up the roster. I know it's a form of cheating, like looking up clues in a crossword puzzle. But everyone does it.

Let's get back to surveying who's here, shall we?

Oh, before we do, one more thing. Let's go back to "Hell hath no fury." Who do you think wrote that? I won't give you three choices because it'd be a waste of time. After all, everyone selects William Shakespeare. But that would be wrong! It turns out the line comes from a 1697 play by William Congreve titled *The Mourning Bride*. I know. They should just assign the line to Shakespeare and be done with it. I guess *The Mourning Bride* is more popular than *Paul Clifford*, but still.

Ok, ok, back to who's meandering about on the floor.

There's Pad Khan, on sabbatical from Oxford University, where he reportedly teaches economics. He's in conversation with Flint Silver, the ex-congressman who suffered an embarrassing defeat in the last election. They both subscribe to supply-side economics, which is out of favor these days.

Silver is slowly emerging back into the public eye to see whether there's an opportunity for another run. While no stories have appeared to confirm the rumor, there is a story circulating on the internet that Silver settled a sexual harassment case during his prior stint in Congress. If that's true, he's finished. He was supposed to do one of the morning talk shows the other week, but cancelled at the last minute, lending credence to the suspicion that he's hiding something.

I also noticed Buck Robison. He's a hulk of a man, a former Heisman Trophy winner and NFL quarterback. In just a couple of seasons in the pros, he created a lot of buzz as a sensational runner, passer, and playmaker. Then he got injured and had surgery. Rather than risk further injury, he retired.

Now he's leveraging his athleticism to vault himself into the political arena. If it's true, he's holding his cards close. Maybe the state house, maybe the U.S. Senate. Some people are even saying maybe the White House. I think that's a stretch, but you can't rule anything out anymore.

While I'm looking around, I pulled out my phone to do a little research. And if a lot of these people have political inclinations, welcome to Washington. Everyone here is either running for office or planning to. Every young congressional aide dreams of becoming president of the United States.

Zara Abadan walked into the room, looking spectacular, per usual, in a chiffon dress with lush blues, reds, and yellows. Primary colors for a primo deal maker, that's what I say. Abadan is my age, mid-30s, but she's far more accomplished. She's got an MBA from GW and a law degree from Harvard. She runs her own investment fund, raising capital for enterprising companies.

And then there was Guido Marsh and Sunny Martinez, an inseparable duo. *The New York Times* did a piece on their wedding at the Salamander Resort & Spa in Middleburg. It talked about how they met in San Paolo, when they both worked for the World Bank. Now they operate their own hedge fund.

Oh, wait! I just spotted TJK. Her head is bent and she is engaged in conversation with...someone. I can't make out who she's talking with, but she certainly appears solemn, pointing a finger in the direction of her conversational partner as though she was thrusting a dagger into that person's chest.

I can hear the evening's luminary, Henry David McLuhan, reciting some poetic lines to a group off to the side.

"Once upon a time," he's saying to a rapt audience, "someone was constructing something in heaven with red bricks. One day a brick slipped off the wheelbarrow, fell to earth, and broke into thousands of pieces along the Potomac River below Four Mile Run. A mason's line was drawn creating straight rows, and a storey pole was planted as a guide to set all of those heaven-sent pieces into beautiful homes, forming a quaint community."

Everyone smiles. They love this stuff. They're proud of Alexandria, which has become a destination city along the East Coast, just like Savannah to the south or Bar Harbor to the north.

Closing a block of King Street to traffic down by the Potomac River has been transformative, in my opinion. It was temporary at first, because of the pandemic. But people liked it, so the block has become a permanent pedestrian walkway. And the development along Robinson Landing has turned the waterfront into a kind of promenade.

I don't live in Old Town. It's too expensive for me on the salary as an assistant commonwealth attorney, even combined with Mai's salary as a researcher with the U.S. Attorney's Office. Our place in Fairlington is actually in Arlington County, on the other side of I-395.

I keep saying "our place" because I am an eternal optimist. But, like I told you, I'm living in the basement of a friend's parents' house.

Enough. Let's mingle.

I negotiate between bodies, dodging elbows and sidestepping flailing arms. I get lost in the shuffle and find myself shoulder to shoulder with Luis Aquila.

Chapter Seven — Squeeze Play

Luis Aquila possesses the physique of Everyman — average height, average weight, average build — yet he always stands out in a crowd. He possesses charisma, that undefinable something that transforms ordinary people into extraordinary personas. Successful politicians possess charisma to a greater or lesser degree. Kennedy, Reagan, Clinton, Obama all had charisma.

Aquila's smile is mesmerizing. He knows it and deliberately wears it like a mask. Even when someone speaks about something serious or sorrowful, he smiles. Regardless of the absence of sincerity that accompanies the smile, it is undeniable that Aquila captivates audiences to such an extent that no one seems to care whether it is appropriate for him to be smiling while someone recounts a death in the family or the demise of a business.

In fact, he is so charismatic that no one pays attention to the words that actually come out of his mouth. He could spout revolution and people would still have said, "I'm voting for that man!"

Others can only hope to possess Aquila's gift. Imagine, 100 percent positivity and 0 percent accountability. In my opinion, it's a politician's dream come true.

As I came alongside him, he was engrossed in conversation with Katlin Ash Brook and Siri Deng. He didn't see me coming, which was why he shared a comment with them that never would have been uttered if he'd seen me ahead of time.

"This is the last time that bitch squeezes me," he said with a smile.

The three are huddled together conspiratorially. He's drinking an Irish coffee. Ash Brook holds a flute glass filled with champagne and Deng has a martini in his hand.

The shape of the flute glass is intended to preserve bubbles and prevent the champagne from going flat. An Irish coffee glass is heat resistant and has a handle so you don't scald yourself while holding it. And the classic martini glass has a wide but shallow conical bowl atop a stem. I'm not sure why that is, particularly since martinis were originally served in cocktail glasses.

"This is the last time that bitch squeezes me" wasn't the only thing that I heard come out of Aquila's lips. He added, "No fucking way I'm going to tolerate the humiliation she's put you two through," smiling all the while the venomous words were uttered.

Inside, I freeze. Did I hear him right? What other word might he have uttered? After all, a single letter in a word — a syllable, a syntax — can make a huge difference. I flipped through the dictionary in my mind. Ditch. Hitch. Pleases. Seizes. None of those words worked in combination. I did hear him correctly.

But that's not all. While he was saying "No fucking way," Ash Brook muttered to Deng, "Despicable. She's carrying out an assassination through guilt by association. How horrid. Just like Jeb Stanley." The words popped out like they were being shot out of a machine gun. Very rapid fire.

But the threesome stopped their conversation cold as I turned their gathering into a quartet. "Hello," Aquila smiled. "Nice to see you, David. How is everything in the Commonwealth Attorney's Office?"

"Great," I said. "Nice to see you too. You are here for *Murder in the Museum*, aren't you? Or am I being presumptuous? At least some of the people here were thrown into the place because of the storm."

"Ghastly, isn't it?" commented Ash Brook. "I am," answered Deng, simultaneously. "Not presumptuous at all," replied Aquila. They all lifted their glasses. Ash Brook's flute sparkled. Deng made a face as he sipped his coffee, having obviously just burned his tongue. And Aquila drained what was left in his glass as though it was last call. And he did it without breaking a smile.

There's an English word for draining your glass of alcohol, but I can't remember it right now.

"I need another drink," Ash Brook said. She turned and started to walk away. It was obviously an excuse because her flute was half full.

Overhearing her, Abadan scooped up Ash Brook's glass and said, "I'll bring you another." It happened too fast for Ash Brook to resist. Abadan turned away with the glass in her hand. Ash Brook shrugged and was quickly pulled into conversation with another constellation of guests.

I focused on Abadan, finding it odd that she felt it necessary to refresh Ash Brook's drink.

"I'll join you," said a voice behind Abadan as she headed to the bar.

She twirled around. "No, I'm fine," she said, attempting to wrestle free of the hand that grabbed her arm.

Flint Silver pressed his fingers more tightly around her arm. "Why did you take away her glass?" he asked. Silver is tall, 6'2", but reedy. He possesses a mane of silver hair streaked with black that cascades over his collar, Bernie Madoff-style. His blue eyes are piercing, his nose aquiline.

"I wanted to disarm her," answered Abadan. "She drinks too much. And please get your hand off me, Flint."

He didn't relent.

According to Wikipedia, flint is a sedimentary cryptocrystalline of quartz. It's durable and chips into sharp pieces. When you strike flint against steel, it sparks. That pretty much described the guy.

He'd been ousted from the U.S. House of Representatives by the voters in the past election. But, in my view, he'll be back in the fray in no time. He'd shown his mettle — no pun intended — in previous bouts for seats in the Alexandria City Council and Virginia House of Delegates, and as lieutenant governor of Virginia. But he'll only prevail if he can make the rumors die down.

He's a brawler. It was the British politician Aneurin Bevan who first said, "Politics is a blood sport," and the saying has no better poster child than Flint Silver, who is a ruthless man who pillories rivals in every election cycle.

In my view, he's driven daggers into the backs of too many opponents. Any politician who thrives on backstabbing, insults, and innuendo makes enemies. Eventually they gang up on you and knock you out of the ring. If you're tough, like Silver, you get up and back into the fray.

As Flint pulled Zara across the hall, I managed to catch a few whispers of their conversation. Seeming slightly alarmed, she asked, "Where are you taking me?"

"Why?" Silver asked. "What's the matter?"

"Nothing," she said. Yet, in the back of her mind, Abadan was probably thinking about a politician whose body had recently been found at McCutcheon Park in nearby Fairfax County.

The man's name was Rodney Caron. He challenged Silver for his seat in the U.S. House of Representatives. It was a nasty run-up to Election Day, with Caron leveling a series of devastating blows against Silver. It wasn't enough to topple him, but it did earn him Silver's perpetual hatred.

Caron's death was ruled a suicide, and social media conjured up comparisons to Vincent Foster, the deputy White House counsel during the Clinton administration whose death in 1993 was also ruled a suicide after the body was recovered in a Virginia park. Like the Foster case, Caron's death spawned a number of conspiracy theories. Many people theorized that Silver had something to do with Caron's demise.

Abadan wrestled to get free of Silver's grip.

"Trust me," said Silver. "My intentions are pure. We're just going to another watering hole." A scowl crossed his face. "And if you're thinking about Rod Caron, those rumors were nothing more than attack ads. They were hurtful to me. They also served their purpose because I lost reelection. I would never do something so stupid. You believe me, don't you?"

Abadan's quivering voice betrayed her uncertainty. "Of course,

I know it's nothing," she said.

Chapter Eight — Dang

I tried to follow Silver and Abadan with my eyes, but they ducked around a corner and disappeared out of sight, with Silver leading Abadan by the hand and both of them engaged in what appeared to be an unsettling conversation.

Meanwhile, Luis Aquila was attempting to carry on some kind of inane conversation with Siri Deng and me. "How's the caseload been in your office?" he asked. The question sounded artificial. "I read about crime going up all around the country. I haven't noticed an appreciable uptick in Old Town, however. Am I mistaken?"

"Yes," Deng chimed in. "Homicides in particular. It's happening in all of our major cities. Chicago, New York, New Orleans."

I assumed the two of them wanted to erase any lingering thoughts in my mind as to what I'd overheard. I played along. "We've been fortunate," I replied.

Deng stood so close I could smell his cologne. It was sweet and fruity.

"We haven't had a single murder in Alexandria this year," I said. Of course, as always happens, you're asking for trouble when you brag about something like that. Within 90 minutes, we would log the city's first murder, right here.

I studied Deng. He was dressed in a purple shirt with an open collar. I guessed he was in his mid-70s. His neck was gnarly like the exposed roots of a mature tree. If I'd been him, I would wear turtlenecks or consider plastic surgery, or both. His skin was thick, almost reptilian, with a greenish tinge.

One area where age spared him was his thick hair. But he abused the blessing, dying his hair some awful garish color that looked totally unnatural, like seaweed. The man was ghoulish and could qualify as a *Batman* villain.

After jawboning for ten minutes or so, I broke free. I slunk off and hid in a corner. Pulling out my phone, I searched Jeb Stanley.

That was the name that Ash Brook mentioned. Jeb Bush popped up. I tried again. And this time I got a hit. It was a news article that said Jeb Stanley, the head of some hedge fund, was stepping down because of his past relationship with Jeffrey Epstein. I don't know about you, but I don't believe Epstein hanged himself on Rikers Island. And I'm not a conspiracy nut or anything like that.

Anyway, I couldn't find a link between Deng, Jeb Stanley, and/or Jeffrey Epstein. But I felt I was getting close. On a whim I searched "Deng sexual accusations."

After a series of strike outs, I got a hit. It was a *Washington Chronicle* article, but it wasn't on the newspaper's website. I found it in some lost and found corner of the internet. It read as follows:

Sex Allegations Plague Philanthropist

by Thomas Mann, reporter, @The Chronicle Newspapers

Siri Deng, who has staked a massive amount of capital in rDNA vaccine development, has been accused of sexual improprieties with female students.

I was stunned. Why didn't I know about this? This was like reading about the parish priest being accused of having sex with underage kids. Actually, that's a bad analogy. Given the sad state of affairs in the church, those stories occur all too frequently.

It's so regrettable and disgusting. I find it particularly offensive because I'm Catholic. I feel bad for both the victims and the institution. It's testimony to the fact that people and institutions destroy themselves from within. So if you want to survive, there's no need to look over your shoulder. Just look in the mirror.

I felt a shudder. That's when it started.

I don't know how it entered my mind, this sense of foreboding. Perhaps it was the weather, which was dreadful. Maybe it was the unexpected and disquieting news about Deng. Or perhaps it was remembering how people and institutions keep crumbling before my eyes. People I admire. Institutions to which I've belonged. I was an altar boy once. I was in Scouts. Now everything is falling apart.

Maybe it's even the crowd. Thirty minutes ago, I was delighting in its sound. Now it's making me nervous. Maybe I'd grown more accustomed to silence and solitude than I thought. In some respects, maybe being alone is safer. I didn't used to feel that way, but I'm beginning to think the pandemic might have done a number on me. Maybe the pathogen entered my psyche.

I like crowds but, let's face it, bad things can happen when people gather. We've seen it at rock concerts, where fans get trampled, and at parades, where people out for a good time singing and dancing get struck by cars roaring through crowds at high rates of speed. Freakish things happen.

Tonight is further testimony to that fact. This should be an enjoyable evening, but it's going to turn into a horrid scene with a body lying in a pool of blood.

Having found this article about Deng unsettled me. But the dark thoughts dissipated a moment later.

Chapter Nine — Here Comes My Man

Mo Katz appeared.

He's tall, dark, and handsome, with slightly graying steel-wool hair, a gracious smile, inquisitive eyes, and a relaxed demeanor. He's always challenging the conventional thinking, which is why he's such a successful lawyer and crime solver.

Mai and I were enthralled by Katz when we first met him in 2017 to crack the Daingerfield Island case. Since then, it's been one adventure after another. There've been some personal losses, especially following the tragic stabbing on Slaters Lane in 2020. And we've had some close calls ourselves. I've been roughed up. But that's nothing compared to what's happened to Mai. She's been threatened, chased, and shot — that's right, shot, and rushed to the hospital. But nothing has deterred her. In fact, it's made her tougher and stronger.

A couple of months ago, Katz was mentioned in an article in *The Washington Chronicle* about multiracial Americans. If you don't know, his father is white and his mother is black. According to the article, one in ten Americans identify as being of two or more races. If you're wondering about total numbers, it's 33 million, according to the 2020 census.

In the *Chronicle* article, Katz talked about how both of his parents tried to "shield" him — his word, not mine — from being immersed in either of their cultures to the exclusion of the other. In their quest for equal cultural immersion — my term, not his — he said that he never really assimilated into either one. As a result, he has this sense of otherness, with one foot in his father's world and the other in his mother's, but not grounded in either one.

Ironically, as he explained it in the article, it's a source of strength for him. He has an innate understanding of people who are disenfranchised from society, i.e. *other*. Plus, people pick up on it and they relate to him. It's enhanced his effectiveness in communicating with people and understanding them.

He's one of the most remarkable people I've ever met. I truly feel blessed and honored to be in his circle...or, to be precise, to have once been in his circle. If I can reconcile with Mai, he'll let me back in. Right now, however, he's playing favorites. He hasn't said as much, but I sense it.

"David, nice to see you," he said. He's drinking a Port City beer. He is actually the only person here who is holding a bottle of beer. "How's everything going?" he asked.

That took a little nerve, to be honest. He knows perfectly well that it's not going well. I know Mai's spoken to him about our separation. In addition, I'm reasonably certain it's made the rumor mill throughout the Alexandria criminal justice system. He's probably concerned for her both on a personal and professional level. After all, these sorts of things can affect your job performance, and Mai is the star research assistant in the office. Although maybe I'm giving myself too much credit here. Maybe it hadn't impacted Mai's performance at all. In fact, maybe she's performing even better with me out of her life.

"Great, Mr. Katz," I lie. "It's going great."

Calling Mo "Mr. Katz" is a deliberate ploy on my part, by the way. I know he's upset with me. I'm trying to be deferential. I normally call him Mo. That's what he prefers everyone to call him, regardless of age or rank. It perpetuates a kind of façade that we're all on equal footing. The truth, however, is that the guy stands head and shoulders over anyone else in the crowd.

"I'm doing fine, thanks," I repeat. "I'm winning all my cases. I'm being promoted to senior prosecutor." Listening to myself, I don't sound convincing. I'm making too much of a deal out of winning my cases.

"The commonwealth attorney better be careful," Mo laughed. "If he's not, you might be convinced to run against him in the next election."

"Fat chance," I replied. "I'm loyal."

Boy, how did that slip out? Bad choice of words. Katz gave me *the look* right away. I've been anything but loyal when it comes to Mai. I needed to change tack fast or I was going to capsize right there on the museum floor.

"It's hard, Mo, I'll be honest," I said. "I screwed things up royally. I don't know if Mai will take me back."

My words hung in the air and we had one of those uncomfortable moments when neither of us is speaking. I was tempted to ask Katz what he thought, but decided against it. Actually, I was afraid to ask him. The man's too honest. And that's ironic in a way. After all, the man's motto is *Fatta la legge, trovato l'inganno,* which means "For every law, there's a loophole."

Think about that!

As a defense attorney, Katz made a living out of subverting the system. As the U.S. attorney, he outfoxes criminals. He's successful because his brain operates on both sides of the street, both as a prosecutor and as a defense attorney.

Katz operates within the system. That's the trick, isn't it? A thief is someone who breaks the law. A prosecutor is someone who upholds it. But a good defense lawyer is the guy, or gal, in the middle who finds the loopholes in the law and drives a truck through them. Ergo *Fatta la legge, trovato l'inganno.* Get it?

"Daydreaming?" asked Katz.

I looked at him admiringly. "I was going to ask you about my chances of getting back together with Mai, but I hesitated because I'm scared you'll give me a really honest answer, and maybe it's not the answer I want."

Katz laughed. He has a mouth full of jewels, not teeth. His mouth sparkles. He's a handsome bastard, I have to admit. I think I have a man crush on Katz, like I have for Billy Bob Thornton. And Katz reminds me of Billy Bob in a way, except Katz is black and taller and doesn't smoke or wear sunglasses. But inside I think the two of them are pretty much the same, at least when I think of the character William Hamilton McBride that Thornton played in *Goliath*.

"I think your chances are pretty good," Katz said.

"Do you mean that?" I asked excitedly. I was encouraged by his answer, in addition to being mildly surprised. Okay, totally surprised.

"She doesn't want a divorce," he confided. "I think she believes your son needs his father in his life. And I think she still loves you."

Like I said, the man is as honest as all get-out.

I broke into a smile, sighed, and took a slug of my drink. "Thank you," I said.

"I'm not playing to your vanity, understand," he said. "If I thought she wanted to end the relationship, I'd tell you. And I'm not sharing anything that she would have expected me to hold in confidence. You asked a question and I gave you an honest answer."

"I understand," I said. "I appreciate your candor." Actually, I was thinking he could stop talking now. I'd heard what I wanted. I was afraid he might add something I didn't want to hear.

"I think you have to prove yourself to her," Katz continued. "Despite everything I said, she's probably on the fence when it comes to making a decision."

"Like she's looking for a sign?" I asked.

Katz looked at me as if to say, *No, you dummy*. "Not exactly," he said diplomatically. "You just need to remind her who you are." He hesitated. "Do you remember when I first met the two of you? You were so eager to do the right thing, to pursue justice, to get to the heart of the matter. Remember?"

I did. I got a bit of a lump in my throat. I washed it down with my drink.

"What's happened to you since then?" he asked.

Ouch! Now I was regretting asking him about my chances of reconciling with Mai. I also knew what he'd done, which was set me up! He started out complimentary and honest and everything, and saved the zinger for last. This is a classic trick in a deposition or cross-examination. "Just one more question," says the questioner, suggesting you're about to be let off the hook. The way Columbo would do it.

"What do you mean, 'what's happened?'," I asked.

By the way, that's something I learned from the great man himself. Answer every tough question by asking another one. Parry and thrust.

"People around the courthouse are talking about you," he said. "Even some prosecutors. You're being accused of being haughty. There's some backbiting, to be sure, but I wonder if there's some truth to it."

I have to hand it to Katz. Whenever people string words together like that, they usually say the same thing four times. Like "haughty, arrogant, proud, and vain" or "insubordinate, defiant, disobedient, and disorderly." But he strung together four words that each mean something slightly different. And he drove those words into me like a knife.

"I think a lot of people are jealous of my successes," I replied defensively. I'd suddenly had enough of his truth serum. Time to walk away. Or run, depending on your perspective. "I think I need a drink." I said, imitating Ash Brook's means of escape. "How about you?"

"No, I'm fine," he said. "But what's your answer? Or are you just going to walk away?"

"Am I under oath?" I laughed nervously. I looked for a way out. I didn't see any, although I did spy Zara Abadan handing a flute to Ash Brook.

"Does it matter?" he asked. See, answer a question with a question. Never give an inch to the other side. Do not relinquish the direct examination. Always play the offense, even when the other side has the ball.

"I'm going to get another drink, Mr. Katz," I said. "Nice to see you. Let me know if you need any help with that skit you're putting on tonight."

"I'm not putting it on," he said. "It's McLuhan's project. I'm just playing a minor role. You might ask him whether he needs any help."

I had a premonition then and there that I was going to be playing a role in the play. I didn't know the circumstances and I doubted it was going to be about *Murder in the Museum*, by which I mean the make-believe skit.

Abby Snowe strolled up and took a position between the two of us. I like her. She's very attractive. She appears casual and carefree, although she's anything but those things. She sizes up people all the time. Nothing escapes her. For all of Katz's insights and perceptions, I suspect she puts things on his radar that he totally overlooked. They make a formidable pair.

Right now, I'm pretty sure she senses friction between us. She's come to defuse it, like the bomb squad.

"Hey, David," she said. "I wasn't expecting to see you but it's nice that you're here." She hooked her arm around mine and leaned in. "You've got some fences to mend. Good luck. I'd love for the two of you to get back together."

She said it like it was no big deal. But she and Katz have probably discussed the situation, either between themselves or with Mai, either separately or as a threesome. See how tangled this gets? Yet you'd never know it by listening to her.

"That makes two of us," I said.

She released me and grabbed Katz by the elbow. "C'mon, I want to introduce you to a couple of people," she said.

I wasn't surprised by the quick departure. Like I said a minute ago, I think she noticed I was feeling uncomfortable. It seemed she was doing me a favor.

That's when TJK came into view again. She was in the distance engaged in conversation. I can't make out who she is talking to. I anxiously make my way through the crowd. Regrettably, my efforts were foiled once again, this time by Ash Brook.

Chapter Ten — *Pardonnez-Moi*

Ash Brook guzzles the liquid in her flute.

"Champagne?" I asked, certain that's what I'd noticed her consuming earlier in conversation with Siri Deng and Luis Aquila.

"No," she replied. "Prosecco."

"Oh," I said. I stood corrected.

Both Champagne and Prosecco are sparkling wines. But there are two major differences. For the bottle to be labeled Champagne, it must be from the Champagne region of France. Prosecco comes from the Veneto region of Italy. Furthermore, while both sparkling wines are fermented twice, Champagne is fermented twice in bottles while Prosecco is fermented the second time in steel tanks. Or so they say.

"Listen," I said discreetly, "I have to ask you something very serious." We ducked around a corner. "Earlier this evening, I overheard a conversation in which a comment was made to you about being *squeezed* by someone. What was that about?"

For an instant, I thought she was going to drop her drink. "What are you referring to?" she asked, buying time, trying to find an exit from my inquiry. It was that same technique Mo Katz employed a moment ago. Parry and thrust. Except what did she have to hide?

"You know the conversation I'm referring to," I said pointedly. "Luis Aquila made a disparaging remark about someone being a bitch. He said you and Siri Deng had both been humiliated by that person. And he remarked that he wasn't going to suffer the same fate."

She screwed up her face in a most unpleasant way. Her lower lip curled over her upper lip, her cheeks compressed toward her nose as though she was being pushed on either side of her face, her forehead tightened and drew down toward her eyebrows, which drooped over her eyelids as she squeezed her eyes shut. Was the Prosecco sour? I wondered.

"Go away," she said, dismissively.

"I can help you if someone is taking advantage of you," I said.

"You've got a lot of nerve," she replied, growing more irritated with each word. "First, you have the audacity to eavesdrop on our private conversation. Second, in your quest to acquire more information, you pretend to come to my assistance." Her face was beet red. "I don't like people like that, Mr. Reese, and I particularly don't like you. Now, if you don't mind, get out of my sight."

You might think it wasn't going well between us. And you'd be right. Still, I pressed on. "I'm not trying to interfere in your affairs, Ms. Ash Brook," I said. "I think you're in some kind of danger. I'm only trying to help. The power of the Commonwealth Attorney's Office stands behind me and is ready to support you."

Sometimes I don't know how I get away with statements like that. I mean, I act as though I'm the force of good pulsating in the community. You'd think there was a superhero costume under my shirt. I do overreach. Maybe Mo Katz has a point after all. Maybe others do perceive me as being bombastic and full of myself. Maybe I am. But is that necessarily a bad thing?

Of course, Ash Brook wasn't impressed. "If you want to be helpful, make yourself scarce," she said, turning and walking in the direction of Mari Teller, who was on a collision course with TJK.

Chapter Eleven — Mari, Maddie, Marnie, Mimi

Mari Teller straightened the lapels of her jacket. Her brown hair was tied in a bow behind her head, and whenever she turned, a tail of bushy brown hair flew out from the side of her head. She wore glasses in an oversized frame appointed with fiery red, deep blue, and jet-black mosaics.

Teller didn't need glasses. She wore them primarily to hide the deep circles under her eyes. Plus, glasses masked her dogface features. Someone in the courthouse told me that. I've never actually observed her without her glasses, so I don't know whether it's true.

In addition to a beige jacket, white blouse with a ruffled neck, and long black tie, she wore plaid pants and brown patent leather shoes.

I pretended to be Teller's shadow, staying within earshot while keeping a safe distance.

"Theodora, do you have a minute?" she asked when she encountered TJK.

Teller knew that drove TJK crazy because her name was Theodosia. It was a common mistake, one to which Theodosia was constantly subjected. It's the reason she prefers TJK. Rather than correct people who mangle her name, she's adopted the habit of saying, "Just call me TJK." Problem solved.

"Not right now, I'm afraid," replied TJK. "I just got here. I need to say hello to so many people. Isn't it exciting, Maddie, to finally be able to mix and mingle with one another following that despicable pandemic?"

I guess that's what you call tit for tat.

BTW, did you ever wonder about the origin of that expression? It derives from a 16th century English saying, "tip for tap", that means equivalent retaliation. That's an awesome phrase, *equivalent retaliation*. It conjures up all kinds of legal theories. Our court system doesn't require you to retreat if you're endangered. You can stand your ground, so to speak. That means using reasonable force to repel your aggressor.

"I'm afraid it can't wait," replied Teller. "I know you're trying to avoid me, but I simply can't accommodate you any longer. I feel like a landlord trying to run down a delinquent renter."

TJK took that as an insult, which was precisely what Teller intended it to be. "Running down a delinquent renter, Marnie? Really?"

They moved across the room. TJK was drinking a cosmopolitan from a cocktail glass. Teller cradled a snifter in her palm, sloshing the brandy that floated in the glass. They stopped in a corner of the room, beyond the earshot of others. With the exception of me, that is. I managed to stay close by. I felt something was afoot.

I know. It was only a matter of time before I used the word "afoot" because, after all, every writer models mysteries after the masters. It may interest you to know that "The game's afoot" expression did not originate with Sir Arthur Conan Doyle, the author of the Sherlock Holmes series. It was Shakespeare! That's right. The phrase first appeared in *Henry IV Part I* as: "Before the game is afoot, thou still let'st slip." He also repeated it in *Henry V,* which critics say is one of the greatest historical plays of all time. I have to take their word for it since I've never read it in its entirety. The lines are:

> I see you stand like greyhounds in the slips,
> Straining upon the start. The game's afoot:
> Follow your spirit, and upon this charge
> Cry "God for Harry, England, and Saint George!"

It's fair to say that Holmes' recital is the one that makes the words famous. All I'm saying is that it originated with Shakespeare. Let's be honest, everything originates either from the Bible or Shakespeare.

I strained to hear what Teller said next.

"You've deliberately kept me off the agenda for next month's dedication," said Teller, referring to the dedication of some new venue in the Eisenhower Valley near the U.S. courthouse.

"Whatever are you talking about?" TJK replied coyly.

"I know what you're doing," continued Teller. "You want me replaced by one of your cronies. I've seen how you maneuver the members of the planning committee. You move them around like pawns on a chess board."

"You're trying to steer things in your direction to profit financially from the booming expansion in the valley. Well, I have news for you. I'm not going anywhere. I have allies in all levels of city government. If you think you can maneuver me out of my job, you have another thing coming."

TJK feigned surprise. "Mimi!" she exclaimed. "I'm not trying to push you out of the way. That's a preposterous suggestion. You must, I don't know, be a paranoid schizophrenic or something."

As I'm listening to TJK calling Mari Teller every name that begins with "M" with the exception of her real name, I am reminded of the Beatles song, "I Me Mine," from the *Let It Be* album, which is still swirling around in my head even though I watched that show on Disney+ months ago. And I'm also reminded of M, the head of the British secret service in the James Bond series.

Teller swirled her brandy in her snifter. She stared at the liquor, avoiding looking at TJK. She was boiling mad. If she made eye contact with TJK, she would bore holes through her adversary's head. "Don't lie," she said, her head still tilted toward her glass. "And don't ever talk derisively about me again." She raised her head like a missile launcher cranked upward before its munitions were launched. "The next time you talk to me that way will be the last. Do you understand?"

"Are you threatening me?" TJK asked dismissively.

At that moment, Guido Marsh and Sunny Martinez joined the two women. Marsh held a pint glass with a Port City logo stamped on it. Martinez was holding a lowball glass wrapped in a napkin. A plastic sword spearing a cherry and orange wedge was splayed across the top of the glass. She picked up the sword by its tiny handle, nibbled on the cherry, and dropped the orange slice into her drink.

I moved an inch or two closer to continue to eavesdrop on the conversation.

"It sounds like you two are getting a little testy," said Martinez. "You might want to tone it down a wee bit." She pressed the tips of her thumb and index finger together when she said *wee bit*. "This is a social event, not a brawl."

Marsh and Martinez resembled Sonny and Cher. She was taller than he was. His hair was cut like a Dutch boy's. Her thick black hair hung over her shoulders and down the front of her shimmery gown like a shawl. He wore a black dinner jacket over an open-collared white shirt, tight black pants, and boots with pointed tips.

"Guido and Sunny!" exclaimed TJK. "You appear like two white knights just in the nick of time. Madge was threatening to throw me into the Potomac River if I don't start being nice to her."

Marsh took a slug of beer from his pint and wiped his upper lip with the palm of his hand, massaging a thin bead of beer into his mustache. He made no effort to respond to the statement by TJK about being thrown in the river. That suggested, at least to me, that he didn't oppose the idea. "This brew is delicious," he said.

"What did you get, dear?" asked Martinez.

"The spring fling," he answered.

"No, I didn't ask what you were doing this weekend," she laughed. "I asked, what kind of beer is it?"

All four of them chuckled. She had broken the ice. In celebration, Martinez removed the sword from her drink and took the orange wedge into her mouth, scooping out the flesh with her teeth. She took the napkin wrapped around her glass, dropped the orange rind into it, and balled it up. Then she looked around but couldn't find a place to dispose the napkin. So she held the balled-up napkin in her hand, which she dropped to her side.

Marsh and Martinez appear to be the perfect couple, but it's a façade. He's into men and she's always having some clandestine affair with someone. One of the clerks in the courthouse told me that they sleep in separate rooms.

I don't feel bad sharing that information with you. Marsh and Martinez seem to make it a habit to know everyone's affairs, so what's good for the goose is good for the gander. Knowledge is power, you know. It's why Mo Katz enjoys hearing gossip. You learn a lot about people when you figure out their foibles.

Some people go out of their way to avoid knowing about other people's affairs. By avoiding gossip, they must believe they're immune from it. That's hardly the case. You'd be surprised how many people are curious about what their neighbors are doing every hour of the day. I'm not obsessive like that, but I do make it a habit of keeping tabs on everyone who's a mover or shaker in this town.

And Alexandria is a small town. But, of course, every town is a small town. Boston, New York, Los Angeles. They're all small places, at least to the people who actually live in them.

The same is true of D.C. Each city also has its own DNA. For D.C., of course, it's politics. That's everyone's passion. It's why they're here. But once they settle in, they branch out. Just look around you. There are academics, attorneys, journalists, doctors, all sorts of interesting professionals.

Marsh and Martinez separated from TJK and Teller and moved to another corner. I followed them. But before we leave I want to tell you that I didn't know about the hidden meaning behind the acronym TJK. At least, I didn't know it at the time. Later, after the night's events had unfolded and after the dust settled — or perhaps a better metaphor would be *after the blood dried* — I learned about it.

It turns out some people had disparaging words strung together when they said TJK. Sort of like FJB, if you know what I mean. One was The Jagged Pillbox. No, that couldn't be it. There is no P in TJK. Actually, I can't remember them, or perhaps I put them out of my mind because it ruins my image of her. Suffice it to say, not everyone who referred to Theodosia as TJK did it affectionately and respectfully.

I slipped behind Marsh and Martinez.

"What the hell was that about?" said Marsh. He studied his pint, which was nearly empty. "I have to get a refill," he said.

"Wait a second," Martinez grabbed his arm. "What are you talking about?"

"Mari threatened TJK before we approached them," he said. "I heard her. I know it has something to do with the fact that TJK is trying to push Mari out of that commission. I don't blame her. Mari is anti-development. If you left Mari in charge, we'd revert to the horse and carriage. She's just bad for business. A person like that shouldn't be on a commission of a dynamic city like ours."

"Well, I disagree," said Martinez. "I don't blame Mari for wanting to kill the bitch."

"Shh," Marsh whispered. "That's really uncalled for, you know. You should keep those feelings to yourself. One of these days, she's going to end up floating in the Potomac River, and then what? You'll be a suspect."

"Don't make me laugh," said Martinez.

"It's really not so funny," he replied. "In fact, who knows, it could be tonight."

"Well, as I said, I wouldn't blame Mari. TJK has been spreading false rumors about her in order to damage her reputation and make it easier to force her out. I've actually heard her accuse Mari of ethical improprieties, such as opposing developing a parcel in the Eisenhower Valley because she had a partnership interest in some business and wanted to stifle competition. That was just such BS."

Marsh finished his beer. He looked around, eager to return to the bar.

"What is it?" asked Martinez. She studied Marsh's face. "Oh, no, don't tell me it's the bartender. Do you recognize him? Have you been out on a date with him?" She looked around quickly. "You disappear in the crowd so that he doesn't see you. Give me your glass. I'll get refills for both of us."

I saw them separate. I knew something was up. I wanted to figure it out, but my attention was already elsewhere. I'd spied Zara Abadan again.

As I made my way toward her, I recalled some of those names for TJK. One was The Jaded Killjoy; another was The Jaundiced Knave; and a third was The Jagged Kook. Those are actually borderline imaginative. One or two were worse. I'm not going to mention them out of respect for the dead.

Chapter Twelve — The Z That Stands for Zara

Zara was drinking white wine. The white wine glass is smaller than the one used for red wine. The bowl is not as big and the stem is shorter. Red wine is poured into a larger glass, I'm told, for better aeration. And the stem is so your hand doesn't warm the glass.

Actually, I think that's all a lot of rubbish. Wine doesn't really sit in a glass very long. And, as far as the stem goes, it's fashionable these days to drink wine in a stemless glass, so that pretty much debunks that theory. And red wine is already warm, right?

I've always believed all this silliness about wine glasses is nothing more than a reason to compel people to buy glassware. In college, I used to drink wine out of rinsed-out jars. I never thought about the oxidation.

What is oxidation anyway? I'm not sure but I'm going to wager it has something to do with retaining the lighter notes that are found in white wine. I know, that begs the next question. For that matter, what's a note?

Let me look it up right now on my phone. Here it is. In the wine business, a note refers to "the nuances in flavor and aroma found to include acidity, texture and balance." Okay, big deal. I go back to what I said a minute ago. I used to drink white wine out of jars and it tasted just fine, even if I had to curl my lips over the twist in the top of the jar. To this day, I prefer drinking white wine from a small regular glass without a stem. But that's just me.

"What are you doing?" asked Abadan, brushing up against me. We had a thing once upon a time. It was before I met Mai so you can forget about it. She's sophisticated, alluring, and sweet. A very gentle soul.

"I'm looking up wine 'notes'," I said.

"What for?"

"Curiosity," I said. "You don't associate notes with booze. You normally associate them with music. It's sort of odd, you know."

She shrugged. It was obvious she didn't care. But she also didn't want to expend the energy to even think about it. That's one of the many amazing features about Abadan. Her every movement, word, and act is done with minimal motion. It's like a Zen thing. From the moment she steps into the room, she displays it, like a car in a low gear. She moves about steadily, but there's no wasted movement.

"What's new?" she asked.

"I'm being named deputy commonwealth attorney in a couple of weeks," I said. "That's my big news. I've only been in the office a couple of years. I'm racking up a ton of convictions. Juries love me. All is good."

"How's Mai?"

I shook my head. "Not so good on that front," I said. "I've made a couple of blunders." I can be frank and honest with Abadan. We were close once, so there's a kind of bond between us.

I probably would have maintained our relationship if it had been left to me, but that doesn't mean I don't love Mai.

It's true. Abadan is the one who broke off our relationship, I mean. She never really provided me an explanation. She's like that. One day you're high and mighty in her eyes. The next day you're nobody. She doesn't explain it, but it defines you. If you don't pass the Abadan test, you're out in the cold. We ended up somewhere in the middle.

"Too bad," she said. "I like Mai."

"Yeah, so do I," I said. "That's why I'm here. I just dropped over to see if I could run into her. Casual-like, you know. Bump into her. Strike up a conversation. Win her back."

"Good luck," she said. Then, pointing at TJK, she asked, "What's with her?"

"What do you mean?" I turned discreetly and looked at TJK as well.

"She seems preoccupied," said Abadan.

I hadn't noticed, or had I? Either way, she was right. Looking at

TJK, it was evident that something was on her mind. For one thing, her brow was furrowed. I'd never seen a wrinkle on that face before. It was disconcerting, like a black cloud running across a blue sky.

That wasn't all.

Her lips were turned down at the corners as though someone had taken fish hooks, dug them into her flesh, and pulled down as hard as possible. Her eyes were drawn in slits, waiting for someone to drop nickels through them. And even her complexion was paler than usual, like chalk.

"So forlorn. Bereft of joy. Awaiting pending disaster. Study her face. Something is happening. She feels it. It will be tonight. Her body senses pain. Acute pain. A physical attack."

I thought I was listening to myself. Then I realized that Abadan was stating my thoughts out loud. I'd never heard so many words come from her mouth in one evening, let alone a single encounter. And it was like she was reading my mind.

Up until now, what had she said? Go back and examine the pages. "What's new?" "How's Mai?" "Good luck." Two-word sentences, for the most part. I was the one doing all of the talking. Now she was Zara the Mind Reader.

"Warn her."

"What?" I asked. "You want *me* to warn *her* of a pending disaster? She'll think I'm nuts. I'm not going to do that. I want to maintain my relationship with her."

"There'll be no relationship to maintain if you don't act," said Abadan. "I'm serious. She'll listen to you. You're a prosecutor."

"No." I felt as though I'd stolen a page from her book, responding with a one-word sentence. Granted, TJK did look forlorn and joyless, and that wasn't a look that one normally associates with her. But what was I supposed to do? Point her to the door and tell her to leave before it's too late? Or remain by her side all night, making sure no harm came to her?

"Look, David," Abadan said, cradling her drink in one hand

while pressing the index finger of her free hand into my chest. "You want to impress Mai? Save TJK. Be a hero."

I squinted at her. Usually I'm bold and decisive. I felt immobilized to act.

"Do what you want, but don't come crying to me when she's lying in a pool of blood," she said. "Now's the moment. If you don't act now, you'll regret it tonight and for the rest of your life."

"You do it," I blurted out angrily. "If you think there's some impending disaster, why don't you raise an alarm?"

"Not my style," she said, taking a step back.

We parted company. I wouldn't see her again until I called her to testify later in the night. Nonetheless, I didn't forget our conversation. Later, after the deed was done and the inquiry had begun, I wondered if things would have been different if I had taken Abadan's advice.

I'm not sure what held me back. Perhaps it was fate. Cold, calculating, unfathomable fate.

Chapter Thirteen — Mixing Irish Coffee with a Martini

I stopped at a serving tray in the corner. Among the plates and glasses, an Irish coffee glass leaned against a martini glass. Both drinks were half consumed.

I recalled that Luis Aquila was drinking an Irish coffee and Siri Deng had a martini when I was talking to them. Ash Brook was part of that initial conversation, but she departed shortly after I joined. You'll remember Aquila was making a disparaging comment about being *squeezed* by someone.

Did Aquila and Deng have a sidebar conversation after I departed? If so, did the presence of a small reservoir of alcohol in each of their glasses suggest that they adjourned quickly, perhaps in anger?

What could two men have discussed when they were no longer in the company of their third companion, who was a woman? I wasn't sure, but the first thing I thought of was sex.

What specifically were they discussing? Were they comparing notes about Ash Brook? Unlikely, I concluded. Were they perchance sharing stories of their sexual exploits? Again, unlikely, as neither struck me as a Don Juan.

The greater probability was they were talking about being squeezed by someone who knew something about their personal proclivities.

I know what you're thinking: How could I possibly draw those inferences based upon two glasses sitting on a tray next to dirty dishes and used silverware? I mean, I'm no Sherlock Holmes or C. August Dupin.

By the way, if you didn't know, Dupin was the invention of Edgar Allen Poe, who created detective fiction before Sir Arthur Conan Doyle's Holmes or Agatha Christie's Hercule Poirot appeared in print. Dupin's star has somewhat faded in comparison with those other two criminologists, but he remains the first fictional heavyweight in the genre.

While it's true that I'm no Holmes or Dupin, no master of deduction or, in the case of Dupin, of ratiocination — a term Poe used to describe a combination of intellect and imagination in solving a crime — I know an accumulation of factors when I see them.

From the moment I entered and Michael Charles cast aspersions upon TJK, I have overheard, observed, and researched things that seem to be pointing in the same direction.

I haven't decided what direction that is, exactly, other than one that is pointed away from good and in the direction of evil. Despite dozens of warm bodies in the room, the building is cold. Bitter damp air permeates both the upstairs and downstairs, as though someone left the windows open and gale-force winds are driving cold rain and chilling air through the place. Forces were gathering like dark clouds in the sky.

I wonder if it could have anything to do with the *Female Stranger*. Who, you ask?

She is the soul that some say haunts Gadsby's. If you don't believe me, look it up in Wikipedia. She died on October 14, 1816, at the age of 23 years and 8 months. The inscription on her gravestone, which is in St. Paul's Cemetery in the Wilkes Street Complex, includes the following words:

> How loved how valued once avails thee not
> To whom related or by whom begot
> A heap of dust alone remains of thee
> Tis all thou art and all the proud shall be

Mai and I stumbled upon her grave when we were searching for little Katie Fortune during the Roaches Run case in 2021.

She is rumored to be none other than Theodosia Burr Alston, the daughter of Aaron Burr. We all know Theodosia from the hit musical, *Hamilton*. By the way, and this is really freaky, the street where her tombstone lies is Hamilton Road. I kid you not!

According to legend, the Female Stranger took up residence in the museum. Some people claim to see her silhouette in the window. She protects the vulnerable who visit the building and punishes the evil ones who commit atrocities on the premises.

I myself don't subscribe to such stories, but they're fun, don't you think?

Wait, what's that?

I just felt a tug on my elbow. I turned, half expecting it to be TJK. Wouldn't that be something, if she was looking for me with the same determination with which I was trying to locate her? Except no one was there. At first, I couldn't believe it. I was as certain of the sensation of someone pulling my arm as I am of my own name, David Emerson Reese.

I glanced around. That's when I saw the big bulky figure of a former NFL player. I turned my attention to Buck Robison.

Chapter Fourteen — Kiss Me, You Fool

As I said earlier, Robison is a former college and professional football star. He limps slightly, a reminder of a playoff injury that cut short a promising career, or so I assume. He's moving over toward TJK.

That was odd. I didn't know they knew one another.

But that's not what I found unusual. My attention was piqued because TJK seemed to move away in the opposite direction when she saw him approaching. Clearly, she wanted to avoid him. That's weird, I thought. I kept my eyes glued on them and edged closer.

"You're avoiding me, aren't you?" he asked once he had closed the distance between them. The accusation was directed at her like a guided missile. Others didn't really hear it because it wasn't targeted to them.

"Buck," she said, turning around briskly. At least I think she said *Buck*. It's entirely possible she uttered a slightly different word since she was clearly attempting to slip away.

As TJK turned, she stumbled slightly and her wine sloshed in her glass. Some spilled on the floor. As she attempted to steady herself, Robison came alongside, taking her arm. I moved in even closer, straining my ears to hear their conversation.

"You don't return my calls," he said. "You don't reply to my texts. You don't answer your emails. I even knocked on your door the other night. I knew you were home, but you didn't answer."

TJK did not respond to his accusations. She simply said, "Come with me."

I followed them. As I did so, someone brushed against TJK. I could have sworn the person slipped a piece of paper into TJK's purse, a bulky monstrosity as big as a sleeping bag that she carried over her shoulder.

TJK walked toward one of the two rooms on the main floor that are roped off for display. She chose the dining area. The wallpaper was light blue. The table, with a dozen chairs arranged around it, was set for a meal. Each place setting had a colonial china plate with utensils around it: a knife, spoon, and two forks set on a napkin. In the center of the table was a large serving platter with a fake roast on it. Beside the roast was a long, sharp knife that glistened in the chandelier's light from above the table.

TJK lifted the rope from the stanchion and stepped inside. Robison followed. She replaced the rope and moved to a corner out of sight of anyone who might wander by and look into the room.

Robison hesitated, unsure of himself. TJK murmured, "Come here." The entreaty echoed in the room like a siren's song.

Once he joined her in the corner, she threw her arms around him, pulled him close, and pressed her body against him. His arms wrapped around her waist.

You might be wondering how I was able to see all this without being seen. Luckily for me there was a large glass-fronted china cupboard opposite them that reflected like a mirror. I positioned myself outside the doorway at an angle where I could see them perfectly in the glass. And the room's acoustics favored me as well.

"I've tried to avoid you, it's true," said TJK. "But it's no use. As soon as I see you, my defenses melt."

They kissed. His tongue dug greedily into her mouth. It seemed that time stopped, at least for him.

"That's enough," she said, pulling away. "This is a safe corner but let's not act with abandon." She spoke just in time. Another second or two, and Robison would have ripped off all their clothes, pushed aside the colonial dinnerware, and heaved her up on the table.

"When can I see you again?" he asked eagerly.

"As soon as Vauxhall Mews is settled," she replied.

"That's a stall tactic," he said.

"No it's not, darling," she replied. "Once the coast is clear, we'll go to the Bahamas. It'll be paradise." She looked at him seductively. "Late nights and later mornings."

Robison looked as though he was ready to go home right then and pack for the trip. Open windows in a cool breeze with curtains floating, lying in bed under satin sheets, her body close to him.

"When will it be settled?" he inquired.

"Once I have everyone's signatures on the papers," she said.

"Speaking of which, where are said papers?" he asked. *Said* papers. She scowled. There was no place for frivolity.

"They're in my car," she answered. Then she lowered her voice and they continued talking in a hushed tone.

A sound came from the doorway. They turned. No one was there. Or was there? The discussion ended abruptly and they moved to exit the room.

"I've tried to avoid you, it's true. But it's no use. As soon as I see you, my defenses melt." What was that garbage? I thought to myself. There was no spontaneity to those lines. They were rehearsed.

All I could conclude was that Robison was so madly in love with TJK that he heard what he wanted to hear instead of hearing what was actually said. And I don't mean the words. I'm referring to the tone, cadence, expression, and affectation. Those were all phony. I should know. I do the same thing in the courtroom when I'm addressing judges and juries. I tell them what they want to hear or, more precisely, what I want them to hear.

My point is: It takes a phony to know a phony. And I didn't say pony. I know what I am when it comes to soliciting affection.

And that kiss! Geez. He was smitten. She was bored.

The bad news is that I didn't hear what was said after she said the papers were in the car. I leaned in but it didn't do any good. Fortunately, I was constrained by the rope or I would have tumbled into the room and revealed that I'd been eavesdropping.

I'm going to keep an eye on them, if possible.

As I do so, let me say something about keeping things in one's car. You'd be surprised how many people do that. People leave firearms in their cars, sometimes with a bullet in the chamber. They keep mini file cabinets in their trunks with automobile titles, insurance papers, bank statements, and other items that really should be maintained in a home safe or safety deposit box. Also, on occasion, people keep clandestine documents in cars, like love letters to people with whom they're having adulterous relationships, or private emails.

I know this because it's come up repeatedly in court cases. Obviously, TJK is one of those people. The Junk Keeper. Maybe that's one of the phrases people think of when they call her TJK. I wonder what else she's got in her car.

Chapter Fifteen — Rows and Mews

I turned the corner. Oh, no! Patricia Blu! I desperately want to disappear, but no such luck.

Patricia operates a local boutique. I dropped in there once to buy something for Mai. I struck up a conversation with Patricia and, before I knew it, Patricia and I were entwined in a flirtatious relationship. As you might expect, it had the potential to grow into something more provocative. And it did. Sort of.

"Hello, David," she whispered in my ear in a la-di-da tone.

I smiled wanly.

"You need to drop by the store sometime," she said.

"I will," I said in a tone that meant *not now!* "Nice to see you here."

I attempted to get away, to no avail.

"I almost didn't make it," she continued. "I was at Vauxhall Row on Eisenhower Avenue looking at the models. It's a beautiful development. It's just a shame they're going to tear down a homeless shelter, a dog park, a performing arts center, and a rehab facility to build luxury townhomes."

WAIT!

That's the development TJK was talking about with Buck Robison. At least, that's a fair deduction based upon the limited evidence at our disposal.

Vauxhall Row on Eisenhower Avenue. Does that have a certain *je ne sais quoi*? I don't think so.

Today, it seems as though every apartment building or condo has a hip name. There's the Dylan in Potomac Yard, which is okay, I guess, because, well, it's Dylan. And I'm a Dylan diehard, especially concerning the early stuff. *Highway 61 Revisited, Bringing It All Back Home,* and *Blonde on Blonde* are the trifecta of musical genius. No wonder Dylan was awarded the Nobel Prize for Literature. "Visions of Johanna" alone should have sealed the deal. And how about the fact that he didn't go to Sweden to accept the award. So Dylanesque.

Then there's The Bloom at Braddock Apartments on Henry Street. I guess that's okay too. It's nice imagery. And I like Harold Bloom.

At the edge of Washington Street near the Belle Haven Country Club, there's the new apartment complex, The Thornton. Again, I like it because I enjoyed reading Thornton Wilder in college. *The Bridge on the River Kwai* was a great book.

But, in general, I don't like new apartments and condos having people's names. A residential dwelling should have a special name, like Porto Vecchio, across the street from The Thornton. Now there's a name. Or Marina Towers, off Slaters Lane. I like that too. Sort of classy. They evoke a mood, don't they?

I'm ambivalent about Vauxhall Row. The way you pronounce it. Vaux. It rolls off the tongue in an unappealing way.

Oh, boy.

I just realized I made a major *faux pas*. I didn't mean *The Bridge on the River Kwai*. That was the name of a movie (based on a book by Pierre Boulle) directed by David Lean where the British POWs whistle that tune, the "Colonel Bogey March." I meant *The Bridge of San Luis Rey*. That was the name of the book written by Thornton Wilder.

Sorry. Back to Vauxhall Row on Eisenhower. I apologize for going off on all of these tangents. In my defense, I warned you. It's one of the things about me that drives Mai crazy. And not in a good way. Not like, "David, you drive me crazy! I want to rip your shirt off!" More like, "David, you drive me crazy! I want to pull my hair out!"

However, there is the method of my madness. I do the same thing in solving a case during a jury trial. I go through a host of meaningless theories before I settle on the right one. You know what Sir Winston Churchill once said? "You can always count on Americans to do the right thing — after they've tried everything else." I'm sort of like that. I make a lot of blunders and take wrong turns before I find the answer.

You'll see what I mean later tonight, as I examine the possible suspects of the murder that's going to happen in about an hour. I get everything wrong until I take the right turn and get it right. And that right turn will be guided by the supernatural. But I'm getting ahead of myself.

Back to Vauxhall Row.

Actually, now that I've corrected the error of the bridges over the River Kwai and San Luis Rey, I'm wondering if I've got the correct name for the Vauxhall development. Is it Vauxhall Row or Vauxhall Mews?

What did TJK say? I'd forgotten. I pulled out my trusty phone to conduct a word search.

The first thing that popped up when I input the name Vauxhall Mews is a British automobile manufacturer named Vauxhall Motors Limited located in Chalton, Bedfordshire, Great Britain. It's got a griffin as a logo.

I clicked on the logo, which took me to a different website, where I learned the griffin has been the auto company's logo since its founding in the mid-1800s. Assuming this information is accurate, the company appropriated the 13th century coat of arms of Sir Falkes de Breaute, whose house was called — no surprise here — Vauxhall. The name was eventually incorporated for the surrounding district and, when the auto company was formed in that district, it took the name and adopted Sir Falkes' coat of arms.

That's very interesting. It's also impossible. There is no way that an auto manufacturer existed in the mid-1800s. Right? I mean, I'm not a great student of history, but cars didn't come into existence until the early 1900s.

Aha! Reading on, I see that the company was founded in 1857 by Alexander Wilson in Vauxhall, London, to build pumps and engines. Auto manufacturing commenced in 1903. According to this, the company built a single-cylinder, five-horsepower car with no reverse gear.

Good luck with that!

This is what happens when you search the internet. I think it might be a reason I jump from one topic to another. I get distracted very easily, but who can blame me? The internet is a true rabbit hole. You go there looking for one thing and, before you know it, you've listened to music, watched a sporting event, checked what's streaming on Netflix and Hulu, and bought something on Amazon.

I've closed the automotive website and I'm studying the Alexandria development. I did have the wrong name. It's Vauxhall Mews. Hey, this is interesting! The developer has adopted the same logo as the auto company. There's the griffin, with an eagle's head and a lion's body. It has wings and it's holding a flag with the letters "VM".

I'm no trademark or copyright attorney, but I'll tell you this: Vauxhall Mews had better have gotten permission to use the griffin as its logo or it's going to be hearing from Vauxhall Motors and possibly from the descendants of Sir Falkes de Breaute.

I finally focus on the news articles about Vauxhall Mews, which are downright disturbing.

As far as I can glean from these articles, there is a lot of controversy surrounding the development. The building permit did not comport with regular building and zoning requirements. Several beloved local shops were torn down to facilitate its construction. Local neighbors expressed opposition, but their voices went unheeded.

Yet, despite all of this negative news, the units have been selling like hotcakes for hundreds of thousands of dollars over their asking price. We're talking about million-dollar babies.

The articles don't assign responsibility or blame. If I'm reading between the lines correctly, however, there may have been graft, undue influence, and a total disregard for the concerns of the neighbors.

This seems antithetical to the way things happen in Alexandria, which is pretty much a poster child for good government. Whoever is behind this apparently knows how to pull some strings. And, from what I'm discerning, TJK is in the middle of all of it.

Oh, geez! I've done it again.

Just as I stopped listening to Michael Charles earlier this evening, I haven't heard a word that Patricia Blu's been saying. Focus, David, focus! I tell myself.

"Here's what I think," Patricia is saying as she leans into me. "TJK's used a steamroller approach up to this point. I don't see anything or anybody stopping her. And she seems to have exclusive rights to selling the units.

"As to the demolition? A lot of people don't like to say it out loud, but they consider homeless shelters and rehab facilities neighborhood blights. And the arts center. Let's be honest. There's already controversy about the future of the Torpedo Factory. Who's going to care about the loss of a little shack where they make ceramic pots, right? Not everyone is artsy-fartsy.

"The only real loss is the dog park, but I understand the development has assuaged dog lovers by promising to build a state-of-the-art park to replace the old one."

Blu is not someone you would describe as a compassionate person. And I disagree with her assessment. I think a lot of people do care about shelters for the homeless and venues for artists. You can't let glitzy development run roughshod over everything. If you do, it's only a matter of time before you get pushed aside yourself.

"Listen, it was nice to run into you like this, but I've got to go," she said. "I look forward to renewing our acquaintance. Don't be a stranger, okay?"

She went off. Relieved, I headed elsewhere. Oh, there's Pad Khan.

Chapter Sixteen — This Heart of Stone

Pad Khan was reportedly an economics professor at Oxford University, currently on sabbatical. He is slightly built, hunched, and moves like a guy shuffling down a hospital ward recovering from an operation. His eyes are watery and bloodshot and buried deep in their sockets. However, his frail appearance belied a steely personality.

Oddly, despite his academic credentials, Khan is a courthouse regular, one of those local residents who drops by on a daily basis to check the docket and drop in to watch juicy criminal cases or a particularly nasty divorce proceeding. Most of the other members of that crowd are retirees.

Khan always makes it a point to comment on my work. For example, just the other week, he told me: "You did a good job with that woman when she took the stand the other day, David, but you should have gone for the jugular sooner." He always starts with a compliment and ends with criticism. It's a technique I use myself in examining witnesses: butter them up and then cut them apart.

Tonight, he continued with his commentary about that case, which should have been plea bargained. But the defense attorney was a jerk who made unrealistic promises to a naïve client, probably to boost his retainer.

Fortunately, it was a bench trial. After the judge found the defendant guilty — which was preordained since the evidence was overwhelming and she didn't help her cause when she took the stand and admitted culpability — the case was continued for sentencing. I was pretty certain she'd get community service and be spared a permanent conviction.

Personally, I think minor theft cases shouldn't even be prosecuted. In good conscience, how can you prosecute someone for felony theft with a value of a few hundred dollars when people all around you are robbing the public and private coffers of thousands or even millions for their own aggrandizement? A lot of these defendants in minor cases are needy people with mental health issues, and the amount of the theft is minimal, at least in the scope of things.

It's a lot better to put these folks into a court diversion program and save them a felony conviction, which will haunt them for the rest of their lives. I mean, think about it. If you punish someone for stealing a few dollars by branding them with an F on their chest (for felony), you are guaranteeing they will never be able to find meaningful employment.

I ask you: Is that what we want a criminal justice system to do?

"You should have nailed her, especially after she admitted to the crime," Khan said.

I was annoyed. "I'm embarrassed the case went to trial," I admitted. "Didn't you realize she was destitute? She isn't a criminal. She's just another desperate soul trying to survive."

Khan recoiled. "You sound like a defense attorney or, worse, a bleeding-heart liberal," he said.

That's not an expression you hear very often these days: *bleeding-heart liberal*. First, liberals call themselves progressives. And hardly anyone is accused of being a bleeding heart anything. People are too jaded these days.

Khan shuffled away. I pulled out my phone. I searched his name. One link caught my eye: "Did Pad pad his resume?" I clicked on it. I was directed to Twitter. There was a head shot of Khan in which his watery and bloodshot eyes seemed particularly pronounced. Beneath the photo was a tweet that read:

> OxHouse Professor Pad the Padder Khan-job sells himself as someone other than who he is, which is a fraud and plagiarizer.

Khan told me he was on sabbatical from Oxford. I'm sure of it. And, while I'm not sure where OxHouse is, it's safe to say it's not in Oxford, England.

I went to the Oxford website and typed "Pad Khan" in the faculty search box. There were no hits. I wondered if Pad was a nickname. Then I went to the Economics Department. I searched for professors on sabbatical. No reference anywhere to anyone named Pad Khan. Next, I went to OxHouse. No academic institution exists under that name, at least according to Google.

This is getting weird. Every time I go to Google and conduct some independent research, it differs from the reality that's being presented to me. Frankly, I shouldn't even call it reality. Life is turning into a total fiction. People and places are not what they appear. The closer you look, the further you seem to be from reality.

I needed a drink. I headed for the bar. As I did so, I wondered about Khan, Vauxhall Mews, Mari Teller, Luis Aquila, Siri Deng, and the relationship between TJK and Buck Robison.

I hadn't come here to be consumed with the affairs of others. My mission was a simple one: make up with Mai. I planned to do so while watching *Murder in the Museum*. Now, in a period of less than 90 minutes, my head was spinning as I grappled with tidbits of the private lives of my friends and neighbors.

Was there a common thread? If so, would it be tied together tonight? And, if so, how? On that note, I put my elbows on the edge of the bar and ordered up a Dark 'n Stormy.

Chapter Seventeen — Drinks and Drabs

All right, I know what you're thinking: What's with the drinks? Well, let me try to explain it to you.

All of us identify people in different ways. My brother Teddy, for example, cannot remember anyone's name to save his life. Yet he knows what kind of car everyone drives. When he sees someone, he'll say to me, "There's the guy who drives the Range Rover" or "She's the one who tools around in that red Mercedes."

My sister Hillary identifies people either by their profession or their residence. For example, "He's the attorney who was listed in Best Lawyers in Northern Virginia." Or "She lives in Potomac."

In both cases, my siblings do not know the actual names of these people. They form associations through assimilation, if that makes sense. Whether or not my family's method of identifying people is unique, I do the same thing. Except, in my case, I identify people by what they drink and by the container in which the drink is consumed.

Granted, it's odd. But it's effective.

I attribute this penchant to the fact that I was once a bartender. It's a long story and I won't bore you with the details. Here's all you need to know.

When I turned 18, I got into some trouble with the law. Nothing serious, mind you, and nothing that ended up being a part of a permanent criminal record. In my case, everything got dismissed and/or expunged. If that had not been the case, I might not have gained admission to law school, become a member of the bar, or been hired as an assistant commonwealth attorney.

I think about that all the time. In fact, it's the reason I feel so passionate about helping first-time defendants avoid permanent convictions. *There but for the grace of God....*

To help me keep out of trouble and to separate me from the undesirable elements with whom I was associating, my parents shipped me up to Chicopee, Massachusetts, to live with my grandfather.

That decision, like so many of the decisions my parents made, was riddled with error.

First, the only way to keep me out of trouble was to separate me from myself, which was impossible.

Second, none of my friends were bad influences. The proof is in the pudding: they're all doctors, lawyers, architects, website designers, writers, etc.

And, third, my grandfather was probably the worst person in the world with whom to place me. He was a widower, a drunk, and ran a bar at the age of 80.

And it wasn't just any bar.

The bar was located next to where Mohammed Ali trained for the Sonny Liston fight in '65. I kid you not. The bar was located on Burnett Road in Chicopee. You can look it up. The city tore the joint down after my granddad died. I think there's now an auto dealership on the lot.

But while Ali was training, everyone frequented my granddad's watering hole. Even Howard Cosell, probably. But not Ali. Ali, if you didn't know, did not drink or smoke. He was a devout Muslim.

At any rate, I tended that bar in Chicopee. Despite the fact that the Ali-Liston fight had been decades earlier, the place retained its legendary status. A lot of people dropped by and none of them knew how to hold their liquor. Great remedial education for a delinquent, right? Yet that's where I developed the habit of identifying a person by his or her libation.

"What'll it be?"

"The usual."

I also learned that the glass is as important as what's in it. You don't pour Irish whiskey into a flute glass and you don't pour white wine into a martini glass. This may sound elementary to you, but to me — an 18-year-old who poured every kind of alcoholic beverage he could find in his parents' liquor cabinet into glass jars, mixed it together, and drank it on Friday nights in somebody's parents' garage — this was a revelation.

As a result, in my mind, the person, the drink, and the glassware all melded together.

I should add that Mai doesn't drink. Every time we go out, she asks for water. And not sparkling, exotic water. Tap water. That actually is a good example of what I'm attempting to explain to you. She's modest, pure, unassuming, and frugal. And she stays in total control.

"Dark 'n Stormy, please," I said to the bartender. I felt someone to my left. I turned. I was rubbing shoulders with Monica Livingston, aka Monica Lewinsky, the American actress. I know, you're thinking where did I came up with the description of "American actress" for Monica Lewinsky? Look it up yourself in Wikipedia.

"Did you know the *Murder in the Museum* skit was supposed to start at 8?" she asked. "It's closer to 9 and no one seems to know what's happening. I would have left and gone home except for this rain. We're all prisoners here."

"I'm sure it'll start any minute," I assured her.

Livingston has a small body but inordinately wide shoulders. She is also sort of bald, which I always find disconcerting in a woman. Her scalp is covered with thin strands of hair that are blow-dried to create the illusion of having more hair than is actually on her head. Her cheeks are flushed. At first, I thought it was makeup. Then I realized she doesn't wear makeup. The redness doesn't give her a healthy appearance. Quite the contrary, it actually makes her look as though she needs to have her meds adjusted. Maybe that explains the hair loss. Anyway, tonight she looks especially terrible.

"Are you alright?" I asked, concerned about her health.

"No, I'm not all right," she answered. "I'm cold and I'm tired and I want to go home." She was also half drunk from the sound and smell of things. "I paid a lot of money for a ticket to this rotten show.

Now I understand it's open for free to everyone who's here, which includes a lot of people who didn't pay."

That was weird, you know, complaining about the fact that people were being let in for free to a charity event. I just smiled. My drink was served.

I drowned out whatever Livingston was saying because Pad Khan was seated on the other side of me talking about economics with a group of devotees. I eavesdropped.

"Tossing around all that money during the pandemic caused the inflationary spiral," he said. "That's government for you. First it creates a problem. Then it devises a solution. If government simply left things to the private sector, we'd all be a lot better off."

His comments were greeted with affirmative nods and grunts.

"The shortages in the supply chain have exacerbated the problem, but those shortages didn't cause the inflationary spiral, and they were entirely foreseeable," he continued. "Politicians claim they were blindsided. That's not true. Either they simply weren't paying attention or they're lying."

He took a sip of whisky that he was drinking from a Glencairn whisky glass, which is a specialty piece developed by Glencairn Crystal Ltd. to provide a heightened experience for consuming whisky.

Now I don't mean to be profiling people in any way or to be passing judgment, but I assume Khan is a Muslim name, since it's a common surname for Central Asian and South Asian Muslims, as well as people of Turkic or Mongol origin.

As I mentioned before, Muslims don't consume alcohol, which is considered *haram* or sinful and prohibited. This certainly didn't faze Khan, who swirled the whisky in the wide-bowled glass, smelled its aromas, and continued imbibing the whisky.

"The Federal Reserve's primary purpose for existing is to keep inflation under control," Khan continued. "But, to be honest, the Fed, as it's commonly referred to, bends to the political winds, and

I'm afraid this time it's no exception."

What's with the line *as it's commonly referred to*? Everyone knows the Federal Reserve is called the Fed. I thought that was awfully pretentious. That's like a law school professor saying "SCOTUS, as the Supreme Court is commonly referred to" or someone at a bar explaining "the NFL, as the National Football League is commonly referred to."

In fact, the more I listened to Khan, the more it was obvious that he wasn't really providing any insight. He was reciting something he'd read in *The Wall Street Journal* or the business section of *The Washington Chronicle*.

I pulled out my phone and searched for one of Khan's lectures, copied key phrases and paragraphs, and searched that exact phraseology. Quicker than I could say plagiarism, up popped a column by Greg Ip in *TWSJ*. Bingo! It appeared that Khan simply lifted his lectures from the column.

I put away my phone and continued listening. The more I heard, the more convinced I became that Khan was a fraud. He could have been reading from a teleprompter. He possessed no cutting-edge knowledge about economics at all. How did I know that? Because he wasn't saying anything I didn't already know.

Bells suddenly started ringing inside my head reminding me that everyone here was a fraud or a trickster, or worse.

No, wrong bells. There are actual bells ringing. They're those bing-bong-bing things that inform you the show is about to begin.

"It's about time," said Livingston. "Another ten minutes of this and I would have left, rain or no rain. This had better be good."

Most of the people who were on the main level began to move up the stairs to one of two ballrooms. A few people stayed behind, including most of the people whom I'd spoken to earlier this evening.

Part Two
9:00 to 11:00 p.m.

Chapter Eighteen — *Rhythmic Circles*

"Ladies and Gentlemen, your attention, please. Come in and take a seat."

Henry David McLuhan makes quite an impression, I'll say that about him. He's dressed tonight in white: shirt, tie, jacket, pants, socks, shoes. Actually, they're not shoes, they're slippers. And I think the socks are silk. His hair is also white. In fact, the only thing that isn't white are his earring and rings. They're gold.

Most people entered the ballroom, but some stayed outside, talking and drinking. Chairs were arranged in a semicircle. A copy of McLuhan's book was placed on each seat.

A stage rose from the center of the room. On the stage were a rectangular table and five chairs. A pitcher of water, surrounded by four empty glasses and a half dozen bottled waters, sat in the center of the table. A swivel chair was placed at one end of the stage. A large projector screen was set up behind the table, and a whiteboard stood next to the swivel chair.

"Thank you for coming to hear a reading from *More Rhythmic Cycles*, the sequel to my bestselling book, *The Rhythmic Cycle of Life*," said McLuhan, who seated himself on the swivel chair with a mike in his hand.

Every seat was now taken. The doors closed. Muffled conversation could be heard outside in the hallway and in the adjoining ballroom. The lights were lowered, with the exception of the ones directed at each of the five empty chairs behind the table and the swivel chair on which McLuhan was seated.

"Joining us tonight are Stephanie Erdrich, book critic for The Zebra Press; Wanda Godwin, editor of Alexandria Living Magazine; and the narrators of my two books, Matt Seal and Marsha Swanson," said McLuhan. "Please give them a warm round of applause."

The applause was more than polite. It bordered on thunderous, which was hardly unexpected since both Erdrich and Godwin were well known local writers and Seal and Swanson were popular stage personalities in community theater productions.

The foursome materialized from the corner of the room and took seats on the stage facing the audience. From left to right were Godwin, Swanson, Erdrich and Seal. One seat remained empty.

Even though the event was a fundraiser for the museum, people would have paid handsomely simply to listen to the foursome discuss McLuhan's books. Since *Murder in the Museum* was billed as a parlor game there was a heightened expectancy in the room.

"Stephanie, I wonder if you could provide some context about how the sequel builds upon *Rhythmic Cycle*," said McLuhan.

"Yes, Henry David, but first, let me welcome you to this event and thank you for allowing us to discuss your sequel for tonight's fundraiser," said Erdrich. "Everyone attending tonight's event is being provided a complimentary copy of *More Rhythmic Cycles*."

Everyone applauded. McLuhan stood and bowed. Then he joined the clapping, pointing his hands toward the foursome seated at the table. He resumed his seat.

As the applause receded, Erdrich continued. "The original *Rhythmic Cycle* was a runaway sensation. It postulates that life runs in 12-year cycles and, if you study your own lifecycle, you know when to expect opportunity and when to look out for danger. The book focused upon people. The sequel discusses how this theory applies to businesses, political parties, communities, and nations. It provides insight into how an entity evolves over time, for better or worse."

"Thank you, Stephanie," said McLuhan. "Now, someone give me a topic," he said, challenging the audience.

"The City of Alexandria," hollered a voice. "Explain to me how your 12-year cycle pertains to our fair city."

McLuhan wheeled the whiteboard to the front of the stage. He drew a big circle in the middle of the board. And he wrote down some dates, as follows:

1749

1852

0

1779

1870

"Alexandria was founded in 1749," he said. "Thirty years later, the town was incorporated. Seventy-three years after its founding, Alexandria incorporated as a city, a year off from the top of the cycle, but close enough. Then, 18 years later, Alexandria became an independent city."

He stepped away and looked at the circle. "All of this is significant," he continued. "It shows that the city progresses in an orderly fashion, with events occurring at the top and the bottom of the cycle, suggesting that the city is very symmetrically balanced. This represents efficiency, continuity, and stability."

Everyone clapped. "Astonishing," someone said. "That is so amazing," cooed someone else.

He drew another circle. At the top he wrote "1704" and at the bottom "1746." Then he said, "John Alexander, who was born in 1704, moved to the city that bears his name in 1746, when he was 42. Note the years at the top and bottom of the cycle, replicating the movement illustrated in the previous circle and presaging the efficiency, continuity, and stability that would endure in the community that bears his name."

More applause.

I was standing just inside the doorway, half listening to McLuhan and half listening to the voices outside of the ballroom.

I had to keep my eyes from rolling as I listened to McLuhan. Did people really believe this guy?

I don't mean to give away a magician's trick, but it was totally predictable that someone would ask McLuhan to apply his 12-year cycle thing to the City of Alexandria.

As Katz previously speculated, and I think he's spot-on, McLuhan probably researches dozens of topics in advance of a public appearance, jots them down on index cards and memorizes the info. Then, during an appearance, when a question is asked, he pulls the research out of his memory bank to apply it to his theory. If someone asks a question about something that he has not researched, he simply twists the question in providing the answer, just as is routinely done by any good politician or deceptive witness in a criminal trial.

I removed a copy of tonight's script from my pocket. I already knew what was going to happen. That's a pretty cool feeling, knowing what lies ahead. Of course, who could have predicted what was going to happen in 15 minutes? Nobody. That's not something that anyone had on a 3 x 5 card!

As I removed the script, a paperclip used to keep the papers together slipped off and fell to the floor. I bent down to pick it up. I noticed something else on the floor nearby. It was a piece of paper, begging to be picked up. I walked over and grabbed it.

The paper read: "Meet me Verily at Midnight up in the attic."

McLuhan now asked the audience if there were any further questions. Someone stood and asked: "Where did you come up with the notion of the 12-year cycle?"

Chapter Nineteen — *Murder in the Museum*

I stuck the paper with the cryptic message in my pocket. Then I listened to the performance while reading along with the script. Here's how it went:

Question from person planted in the audience: "Where did you come up with the notion of the 12-year cycle?"

Henry David: "It just came to me."

Patricia Blu, in audience, stands. "That's not true. You stole the idea from me."

One or two of the panel members fill glasses from the pitcher on the table.

Henry David ignores Patricia. "As I was saying, the stories just flowed. I felt as though I'd been visited by my muse."

Patricia faces the audience. Raises her voice. "That's not true. I'm an aspiring writer. Mr. McLuhan offered to help me. Instead, he published it under his own name."

Matt: "That's quite an accusation. Any comment, Henry David?"

Henry David: "I don't know that woman. I've never seen Ms. Blu. I've had a lot of spare time to write during the past four years. I've devoted myself to writing. Let's move on. Matt, would you please read a selection from *The Rhythmic Cycle of Life*? By the way, Matt, is it true that you once lived about a block from here?"

Matt: "Not a block away, exactly. Across town."

Matt narrates a section of *Rhythmic Cycle*.

Patricia: "Excuse me. I was promised the opportunity to narrate this book in exchange for letting Mr. McLuhan appear as the author. I should be up there reading."

Henry David: "Miss, I'm going to have to ask you either to be quiet or to leave."

Matt: "I've never spoken to this woman before."

Patricia: "That's not true. We met one another just around the corner from here, down by the Torpedo Factory."

Matt: "I'm really not that familiar with Old Town. I don't even know where the Torpedo Factory is located."

Henry David: "Ok, look, let's just leave it there. Marsha Swanson, great to have you on the program. You've narrated the sequel to my book."

Marsha: "Yes, that's right." Addressing the audience: "Henry David reached out to me and, after negotiating with his agent, I agreed to read the book for a fee."

Henry David: "Marsha, can you please do a reading for us?"

Marsha reads a page from the sequel, *More Rhythmic Cycles*.

Patricia, standing again: "Excuse me. When you were negotiating with the agent, was there any mention of me?"

Henry David: "I'm sorry Miss, but you keep interrupting. I'm going to have to ask you to leave."

Marsha: "No, Henry David, it's fine." Marsha addresses Patricia. "Yes, as a matter of fact, the agent did mention you. As I recall, the agent said that you collaborated with Henry David on writing *Rhythmic Cycle*. If I remember correctly, the agent said you were going to get a portion of the proceeds from sales of the audiobook." Marsha turns and says, "Wanda?"

Patricia steps to the front of the table and addresses the crowd. "I don't mean to be disrespectful, ladies and gentlemen. But the truth is that this man is a fraud. He never wrote these books. He's collected royalties for these stories. You heard Ms. Swanson say that he was going to pay me a percentage. I never saw a penny for my hard work. I've never seen my name on the covers of these books. I've never received any credit for all my labor."

Henry David: "Miss, would you like to join us at the table? Maybe you can contribute to the discussion, particularly if, as you say, you wrote the books." Patricia takes the unoccupied chair at the table. "Would you like something to drink?" Patricia asks for water. Wanda gives her a bottle of water. "Maybe you can tell us about your version of the origin of the 12-year cycle?"

Patricia: "Absolutely. First of all, Henry David didn't have a vision about the 12-year cycle. I actually did a thesis on it for my doctorate. And I told him all about it when we had dinner together at a restaurant on King Street less than a year before its publication."

Stephanie: "Henry David, I'm shocked at what I'm hearing. I've written about your books in *Alexandria Living Magazine*. And I know Wanda's done the same in *The Zebra Press*. We never would have given you such praise if we'd known you'd stolen the idea from this woman. Did she really invent the theory of the 12-year cycle?"

Henry David: "Stephanie, do I really need to defend myself? I'm the author of these books. I've worked long and hard and I'm not going to have my reputation sullied now by this woman, Patricia Blu, who I've never met before."

Patricia stands. She takes a drink of water from the bottle. She becomes unsteady on her feet. She sits down. Then she collapses and her head crashes down on the table with a thud.

Actually it wasn't her head that made the thud. It was Judge Seal's foot. He slammed it on the floor as Blu lowered her head. Nonetheless, everyone jumped. It was like a gun going off, it was that loud. Seal, Erdrich, Godwin, and Swanson stood up, took a step back, and gasped in unison. It was very well choreographed. And Patricia Blu was outstanding.

Erdrich produced a pillow and placed it under Blu's head. A spotlight remained trained on Blu's form, which was very dramatic, particularly since her hair swept across the table, Medusa-like. I glanced back down at the script, which read:

Stephanie, Wanda, Matt, and Marsha crowd around Patricia.

Wanda: "She's dead!"

Henry David: "Dead!" Looking at the audience. "Okay, folks. Everyone gets a refund. We didn't expect this to happen. Nothing to see here. Now. Just leave."

"Not so fast!" thunders a voice from the back of the room.

I looked up. Mo Katz had just uttered those words. The Sherlock Holmes of Old Town was in the house. He was standing practically right next to me. Like Holmes, he was going to solve the case.

Chapter Twenty — Mo than Meets the Eye

The audience turned. Everyone knew Mo Katz, by reputation if not personally. The man's a living legend. Just the way he said, "Not so fast." It had so much gravitas.

I went back to the script, looking up from time to time to watch, sort of the way you stream a television series in a foreign language.

Henry David: "Who are you?"

Mo: "I'm Mo Katz." He addresses the audience. "Ladies and gentlemen, we've got our work cut out for us. There was an uncomfortable truth being exposed here tonight, or so it appears, because someone decided to silence Patricia Blu by poisoning her." Mo turns to the stage and addresses the speakers. "That someone is one of you. That's right, someone up there poisoned Patricia Blu's drink. And we're not leaving until we figure out who it is!"

Katz turns back to the audience. "Will you help me question the suspects so we can figure it out together? Raise your hand if you'll help me."

Patricia raises her hand. The hand falls back down by her side.

The audience laughed. It was a nice touch, along the lines of *Weekend at Bernie's*. I always liked that movie. It's up there with my favorite comedies, including *A Fish Called Wanda* and *Romancing the Stone*.

Back to the show.

Mo: "Before we begin, however, let's take a vote. I think we have three likely suspects. How many of you think the murderer is Henry David? How many think it's Matt? And how many think it's Marsha?"

Practically all of the hands responded to Henry David. Only one or two thought it was one of the other two. I couldn't see how they factored into it, but we'll see.

Mo: "Henry David McLuhan, based on our informal survey, the overwhelming majority of people think you're the murderer. So, before I begin asking you questions, is there anything you want to say?"

Henry David: "No, except that I never met this woman."

Mo: "One thing I remember Patricia saying was that she met you in a restaurant on King Street. We contacted every single one and there are a lot of them. We asked them to run their credit card receipts against your name. It turns out that you dined there nine months prior to publication of *Rhythmic Cycle*. A waiter remembers you. He said you dined with a young woman who met the description of Ms. Blu. What about it, Mr. McLuhan?"

Henry David: "I eat at a lot of restaurants. I dine alone sometimes, and other times with guests, both men and women friends. Obviously someone saw me dining with someone who looks like her. It's sheer coincidence."

Patricia raises her arm and gives a thumbs down.

Mo: "Let's go to the next suspect." He turns his attention from Henry David to Matt. "Matt, at one point, you said you used to live near Gadsby's Tavern Museum. But, later, when the Torpedo Factory was mentioned, you feigned ignorance and said you weren't familiar with Old Town. Which is it?"

Matt: "I lied the first time. I am familiar with Old Town. I used to live near Slaters Lane. And I'm familiar with the Torpedo Factory. But I didn't poison Patricia."

Mo: "Why did you lie?"

Matt: "I didn't mean to, honestly. It's just that that it seemed as though Patricia was accusing everyone of everything. I was scared. I panicked and told a fib. But I'm being totally honest now. I don't have any reason to silence her."

Mo: "Are you lying again now so that we give you a pass on the murder? I wonder. But let's turn to our third suspect, Marsha."

Marsha: "Look, I don't even know why I'm a suspect in this case. I didn't lie about anything. I've never met Patricia Blu, and that's the truth." Blu raises her hand and gives a thumbs up. Marsha continues: "Like I said, we were splitting royalties." She turns to Henry David: "Isn't that right?"

Mo: "Wait a minute. I'm asking the questions." He addresses Henry David: "Isn't that right?"

Henry David: "Marsha's correct. There was an arrangement to share royalties. And I did know Ms. Blu. We did dine together at the restaurant on King Street. I convinced her that I could market the books better than she could and that I could make us more money if the books were sold under my name."

Mo: "So you killed her to avoid sharing profits."

Henry David: "No."

Matt: "Then you did it because you didn't want to reveal the fact that you're a fraud; that you're really not the author of these books after all. I wish Patricia was alive to sign my copy!" Patricia raises a hand holding a pen.

Wanda: "This has been too distressing for me. I'm leaving." She gets up and exits.

Mo turns to the audience: "Our thanks to the audience, who identified

Henry David McLuhan as the culprit in the initial voting. Are you satisfied that we've caught the real murderer?"

The audience roared its approval. They were sure they got the right guy. But they were in for a surprise. I knew. I had the script in my hands.

Henry David: "You have to believe me. I'm innocent."

Mo: "Actually, Henry David, I do believe you." Mo turns to Marsha. "Marsha, earlier, when you were talking about royalties, you started to ask a question. To whom were you posing that question?"

Marsha: "Wanda."

Stephanie and Matt utter together: "Wanda? Where's Wanda?"

Wanda is no longer in the room.

Matt: "Someone go and find her. I think she has a little explaining to do."

Stephanie asks: "Marsha, was Wanda your agent?"

Henry David: "Wanda negotiated the contracts with the narrators for my books. She worked out the deals with Marsha as well as with Matt."

Marsha: "That's right."

Matt: "Same here."

Patricia raises her hand and gives a thumb's up.

Wanda comes back into the room.

Mo: "Well, it sounds like you have a little bit of explaining to do."

Wanda: "I don't know what I can tell you. I negotiated the contracts with the narrators. So what? They got their percentage of the royalties. It's a standard 9 percent."

Henry David: "Nine percent! You told me they got 20 percent. You and I split the remaining 80 percent, fifty-fifty, with each of us getting 40 percent. If the narrators only got 9 percent and you and I split eighty percent, what about the remaining 11 percent?"

Wanda: "I refuse to say anything until I've spoken to my lawyer."

Mo faces the audience. "Wanda had a motive. She played everyone else to her own advantage. She knew Patricia was in the audience and she was afraid that Patricia was going to raise a fuss. So she brought a bottle of water filled with poison. At the appropriate time, she gave it to Patricia. Ladies and Gentlemen, I think we have our murderer. Will somebody please contact the Alexandria Police Department?"

Patricia begins to move.

Stephanie: "I think Patricia's alive! Maybe there wasn't enough poison to kill her. Thank God, it looks like she's going to be all right."

Mo: "Whoever's contacting the police, tell them we've got a suspect to hand over to them for attempted murder."

At that instant, a scream pierced the air. It came from outside the room. It was worse than the sound of screeching tires before a crash or the sound of gunfire, both of which I've heard in my time. I surveyed the room. My eyes locked with Michael Charles. His eyes displayed a frightening sense of alarm.

The unimaginable had occurred.

Chapter Twenty-one — The Dirty Dozen

The scream didn't seem to stop. It travelled through the rooms, around the corners, along the halls, and down the stairs. It moved as water might if a river ran through the place, drowning us in fright and dismay.

People put their hands over their ears, hearts, and mouths; clutched their pearls; checked their wallets and their purses; blessed themselves; and touched their foreheads for fever.

Soon the whispering began. Quickly it became a murmur. That was followed by howls. A museum staff member had discovered TJK's lifeless body lying in a pool of blood.

"Call the police," someone said. A half dozen people immediately raised their phones and punched 911 into their cell phones. The dispatch center at police headquarters must have short-circuited.

"Bar the doors," someone else hollered. "The murderer's got to be in the museum."

"That's true," someone else said. "Let's figure it out ourselves!"

Suddenly, a hundred guests were thinking the same thing. *Let's solve a murder!* And not just a phony murder, but a *real live* murder.

That's an oxymoron, isn't it? A live murder. Still, you know what I mean.

Some people felt a titillating sensation. *Oh, what fun!* Others displayed a solemn and grim visage. *Upon me falls the burden of uncovering the harsh truth!* To others, there was a look of disappointment. *Can't we just call it a night and go home?*

I didn't think it odd. After all, people react differently to death, particularly when it's not their own or that of a loved one. Some people cry. Others rejoice. Most spend a moment reflecting and then move on.

I fell in league with those who wanted to get to the bottom of the case. And I knew just the person to lead the inquiry. Sorry to inform you, but it wasn't Mo Katz. It was me!

*

"No, absolutely not," exclaimed Katz a minute later. "We can't conduct an inquest here, not tonight. We can't sequester witnesses or put them under oath or do anything like that. We've got to wait until the police get here and conduct a thorough investigation."

"We can do this, Mo," I said. "We can do it the same way you just performed the skit. We can have the suspects take the stage." Notice I had lapsed into the less formal *Mo* rather than *Mr. Katz*.

I had no desire to conduct interviews on the record. I mean, think about it. What if our inquiry actually resulted in a confession? Can you imagine what might happen next? There could be motions to suppress the confession based on the argument that we'd subjected witnesses to custodial interrogations without providing *Miranda* warnings.

Everyone was technically free to leave, of course, although the weather made it impossible to do so. And, as a city prosecutor, I'm an officer of the court; that might qualify me as a bone fide law enforcement officer for purposes of a Fifth Amendment challenge. I'd need time to do some legal research before I'd feel comfortable providing an informed opinion on the matter.

As I saw it, the best course of action was simply to proceed with interviews on an *ad hoc* basis and see what happened.

Maybe, if we were lucky, the killer would confess and we'd be done with it.

"We *can* do this, Mo," I repeated, this time with genuine feeling.

"How?" Katz asked. "There are 200 people here tonight. You can't possibly identify a pool of likely suspects."

I couldn't believe it. He was actually considering my suggestion.

"Yes, we can," I announced. "About 160 of these people were in the ballroom listening to you and McLuhan put on *Murder in the Museum*. That means there were 40 or fewer people outside the room. They are the most likely suspects because the murder probably took place as the skit was being enacted. If you give me ten minutes,

I'll line up a dozen likely suspects to be interrogated."

He gave me a critical eye.

"Interviewed," I corrected myself. "I'll line up a dozen people to be interviewed."

I could sense the wheels turning inside his head. His body twitched a little, particularly his hand, like a gunslinger itching to draw. His dark eyes penetrated the walls of the museum, or so it seemed, as though he was searching crevices of the building for a killer.

"The evidence is fresh," I said. "Emotions are raw. There's been no time to develop alibis. Everything is on the table. We'll never have another moment like this. It's a prosecutor's dream. Let's round up the most likely suspects and grill them. Maybe we come up empty-handed. But maybe we strike pay dirt."

He shook his head ever so slightly.

"We can do this," I said confidently. "Now. Tonight."

"Okay," he said reluctantly. "The first order of business is for us to separate the people inside the ballroom from those elsewhere in the museum. Then we'll issue an order for no one to leave the building. You've got ten minutes to develop a list of likely suspects."

Piece of cake. All I needed was five minutes. And Mai's assistance, which she was happy to render, jumping on a laptop and conducting a series of searches of the guests.

While Katz went off to handle the logistical issues, I focused on the murder suspect list.

I was correct in my calculation that 40 people were outside of the room where *Murder in the Museum* was unfolding. If TJK had been killed in the last 30 minutes, it stood to reason that someone outside of the room was the murderer. Because I was positioned at the doors, I knew no one joined late or left early.

Of those 40 people, I eliminated 16 of them based on research quickly and expertly performed by Mai. Those 16 had no connection to TJK or Old Town. Several were from out of town. I operated on the assumption that the crime was either one of passion or revenge and motivated by a local issue.

Sure, it was possible that it was a random act of violence or part of an elaborate scheme, but those possibilities seemed unlikely and I discounted them. Granted, nothing is impossible given the times in which we live. Just look at the slashing on that London bridge or on a Tokyo subway. Nothing can be assigned a zero probability. Still, I worked off percentages. The lower the likelihood, the higher the probability of dismissal.

Another six were eliminated due to infirmities. For example, two people were in wheelchairs. And four had neurological issues, such as Parkinson's. Those people were accompanied by a partner or caregiver who assisted them in getting around by holding their elbow or directing their movement. I simply couldn't envision them assisting the infirm person in committing murder.

I dismissed another eight on their profession, which included law enforcement, military, medicine, mental health, and academia. I know what you're thinking. A cop is just as likely to kill someone as an ex-felon. Except that's not exactly true, at least not based on statistics. People with security clearances and professional licenses are less likely to commit crimes than people with criminal records. Again, I was playing the percentages. Sure, there was a possibility that the murderer was slipping through my fingers, but the likelihood was remote.

The remaining ten were dismissed for an entirely different, though no less risky reason, in my judgment. They were dismissed based on instinct. This is not to say that anyone can do anything under the right set of circumstances. But if I had to trust my gut, now was the time.

As a prosecutor, I've seen people lie, cheat, bash their cars into other vehicles, set neighbors' trash on fire, stick their dirty paws under coworkers' bras, lift bric-a-brac from friends' homes. I could go on. I'm not saying these ten were incapable of committing a crime, even murder. However, on this night, in this place, against this person, I didn't see it.

Anyone in law enforcement has to trust their instincts. I do it during jury selection and cross-examination. I even do it when I'm interviewing "victims" of crimes. Over half of good police work is instinctual, in my opinion.

I probably violated some OSHA, labor, or civil rights regulations, but I was on a mission to develop a list of potential suspects. I ended with 12, all of whose names are familiar to you: Teller, Aquila, Ash Brook, Deng, Hill, Livingston, Khan, Silver, Robison, Abadan, Marsh and Martinez.

None of them was in the ballroom during the skit. Each of them had the opportunity to commit the crime. And earlier tonight there was something about what they said or did, or how they looked, that gave me pause.

I placed each of their names on a piece of paper, added the juicy tidbits which I'd picked up earlier in the evening, and ranked them in order from most to least likely, similar to the poll that Mo Katz conducted of the fictitious *Murder in the Museum*. I wasn't sure whether I was going to have to interview all of them to get to endgame. Maybe someone would crack early in the game.

The guests were standing or sitting in small clusters, talking about the turn of events. Some were having their copies of *Rhythmic Cycle* signed by McLuhan. Others were looking out the windows to check on the weather. The fierce rain continued unabated.

Chapter Twenty-two — The Murder Room

While I was busily preparing my list and checking it twice, Mo Katz investigated the murder room and later told me what he'd found.

The upper level of the museum housed a series of tiny rooms. There were ten doors along the hallway, five on each side. Behind the doors were four square rooms, four rectangular rooms, and two rooms at the end of the hall shaped like triangles. The five rooms facing the street had windows; the rooms bordering an interior courtyard did not.

TJK's body lay splayed across the floor in a square, 8⊠ x 8⊠ room. The room had a window facing the street. A yellowish light dangled on an extension cord hanging from the ceiling in the middle of the room, barely illuminating the gory sight.

The body was facedown in the center of the box-like room with a hand or foot pointed toward each corner like the directions on a compass. At first glance, it appeared staged. Katz concluded it was the way she fell, unsuspecting and completely off guard.

A large hook had penetrated her carotid artery, causing instantaneous death.

The room was filled with other sharp items: ice hooks, ice picks, and assorted cutlery. I know what you're thinking. *Of all the gin joints in all the world....* There was a sign on the door to the room reading DO NOT ENTER.

Katz found a couple of off-duty cops who were attending *Murder in the Museum* and posted them outside the door with strict instructions that no one should be admitted and nothing should be disturbed.

Then he went up and down the hall, opening and inspecting each room, some of which contained unopened boxes and surplus chairs. Others contained decorations for various holidays: skeletons and tombstones; bunnies and colored eggs; four-leaf clovers and leprechauns; reindeer and a Santa Claus; and turkeys and pilgrims.

The room where the murder occurred was obviously the one that stored dangerous objects. TJK either hadn't read the DO NOT ENTER sign or hadn't heeded it before she stepped inside. If she had entered the room with the holiday decorations, the outcome might have been entirely different. No one would ever know for sure.

At the end of the hall was a wooden staircase that ran down the back of the museum like the spine of a brick-and-mortar creature. Katz walked down the wooden stairs. At the second floor, there was a connecting door. He opened it and followed a hallway to the tavern. He returned to the rear staircase and descended to the dimly lit basement.

On his way, he identified two more officers and asked them to guard the front and rear staircases. No one was permitted to go beyond the second floor. Then he returned to the murder room to conduct a more thorough examination.

Chapter Twenty-three — The 2 Ms

"Ladies and Gentlemen," I began. "Your attention please. Take your seat. We are about to get underway."

As soon as I uttered those introductory words, it occurred to me that I was imitating Henry David McLuhan. Mine was an act, just as his had been. The stakes were higher since I was searching for a murderer, but our techniques were the same.

We both employed smoke and mirrors to get the desired result. In McLuhan's case, it was to make people buy his books. In my case, it was to persuade the assemblage that we had successfully identified the person who had killed TJK.

McLuhan's entire presentation had been scripted tonight. I'd followed along, reading it as I watched the performance. It was like playing sheet music. The highlights, or high notes, were accentuated.

Throughout the evening, I had noticed inconsistencies and ambiguities in what people said to me and to one another. Unconsciously, I had recorded those items in my mind, like highlights. Now, if I could remember them, I could apply them to my examination.

The question, of course, was whether I could pull out those items from my head like items on an index card. Was I crafty enough to draw out their inconsistencies and ask them to clarify their ambiguities? Was I up for the task?

The Dark 'n Stormys that I had consumed weren't helping matters. I mean, this would have been malpractice in a court of law, questioning people on an empty stomach after consuming a fair amount of alcohol.

Maybe if I asked the assemblage for their assistance, they would cut me some slack. And so I continued, "Tonight I am going to need your assistance. I need you to be attentive, insightful, perceptive, inquisitive, and judgmental." I cleared my throat. "We have the opportunity tonight to do something spectacular. Together, we are going to bring a murderer to justice.

"In order to do that, we are going to ask some people to come forward and tell us where they were tonight and what they were doing," I continued. "And, in the process, the murderer or murderers will reveal himself, herself, or themselves to us."

Now you might think that people would never consent to *take the stand,* so to speak, and allow me to question them as to their whereabouts tonight and their relationship with TJK. In fact, I was wondering about it myself. But we would be wrong if we expected any pushback. No one refused to *testify,* as it were.

I have a theory as to why that was. Four names come to mind: Elizabeth Holmes, Travis McMichael, Kyle Rittenhouse, and Jussie Smollett. Each of them testified under oath last year in highly publicized trials. As a result, I think some people believe it's strategically wise to testify on your own behalf.

First off, you control the narrative, or at least part of it. If you don't speak up, others are going to interpret your actions for you. Furthermore, people expect you to testify. Otherwise, they think you're hiding something from them.

Given the recent wave of high-profile cases in which defendants have testified, some people might actually think you're obligated to testify. Of course, no one accused of a crime is obligated to give testimony. The right to remain silent is protected by the U.S. Constitution.

Some pundits assign the willingness to testify to social media. While social media is intrusive, it enables you to project a self-image instead of relegating that role to, say, the mainstream media. Regardless of whether these theories are accurate, no one resisted my request to testify. In the end, they all testified, with one or two exceptions, as you are about to see.

As I indicated a moment ago, I had narrowed the list to 12 people. They were my *Dirty Dozen.*

Where to begin?

Earlier, I'd written their names in order, from most to least likely. I thought I'd start from the outside and work my way inward. It was like weaving a web.

I decided to begin with Marsh and Martinez. They seemed like too goofy a pair to commit a murder. They fumbled and bumbled about tonight. Sure, there was some animus expressed toward TJK. There was even that comment about her body floating in the water. But I just didn't see those two as murderers.

I called their names and they stepped forward. I had never questioned two witnesses at the same time. Two chairs were placed in the "witness box" hastily constructed in the center of the room.

I was anxious to proceed. But my hopes were instantly dashed because, at that instant, a man I did not immediately recognize stepped through the door and called for a halt in the proceedings.

I was stupefied. Who the hell had the audacity to interrupt me, particularly as I was about to begin? Then I recognized the man. I'd seen him around the U.S. Attorney's Office. He ran a surveillance unit of some sort. I wondered what the heck he was doing here.

"Sir," I said.

You might think I didn't address him by his actual name for fear that he might be working undercover. Actually, that never entered my mind. I'd simply forgotten the guy's name. However, I did remember that he was known only as "Mr. Big Stuff" around the courthouse. He was always very bombastic, with an air of self-importance that came across as pretentious.

"Can you please explain your reason for intruding upon our proceedings?" I asked. I tried to act very formal, hoping he'd get the message and buzz off.

Quite the opposite occurred. He grabbed me by the lapel and started to pull me into the hallway. How embarrassing!

Here I am, about to launch into my inquiry. Not only does he interrupt me, but he lays his hands on me. Something like this runs the risk of destroying my credibility. And I haven't even gotten started.

As everyone knows, perception is everything. You can be a complete f-up, but so long as you are perceived as being effective, you're okay. Conversely, you can be a mastermind — the courtroom equivalent of that mad strategic genius Bill Belichick — but, if you are perceived as somehow being inadequate, your credibility is shot and you might as well just get off the stage, grab your things, and go home.

Recalling H.G. Wells' sage advice, "Adapt or perish," I disentangled myself and, turning to the crowd, said: "An important issue related to the investigation has taken precedence over the examination of our witnesses. This demands my attention. I will return in a minute."

All I was doing was saving face.

We retreated to a far corner in the hallway. "What the hell are you doing?" I asked, irritated. "And how'd you even get here?" After all, a monsoon raged outdoors, trees were falling like matchsticks, and roads were blocked.

"I launched an amphibious expedition," he replied, grinning slyly. "I conjured up an entire flotilla." He grabbed my lapel again and pulled me close. He bore a resemblance to John Goodman, the actor. He was oversized and sloppily attired, with a large pizza face and huge hands that resembled baseball mitts.

"Listen," he said, lowering his voice. "You can't examine these two people. They're informants. You'll blow their cover. You have to get them off the stand immediately. Plus, they didn't kill TJK."

"How do you know?" I asked. I agreed with him, of course. After all, they were at the bottom of my list. Yet if my gut instincts were the same as Mr. Big Stuff's, then it might be prudent for me to reconsider my own.

"They don't have it in them," he said. "They're basically a couple of cowards. As soon as we busted them, they cracked like a couple of eggs."

Then another question entered my mind. "How do you even know about the murder in the first place?" I asked.

"It's all over the internet," he said. "Your audience has posted on every imaginable social media. People are taking bets on who's going to be found guilty. I think there are odds from Vegas already."

I pulled out my phone and searched for Gadsby's Tavern Museum. He wasn't exaggerating. The case had gone viral. Vegas already had a line. Zara Abadan was running at 5-3 odds. What was this? The Kentucky Derby?

As I scrolled through my phone with dismay, he continued explaining the situation. "The M & Ms are unindicted coconspirators in a court filing," he said, "but it's all a subterfuge. They're actually cooperating with us."

"I can't just let them loose," I said. "They're suspects." I looked at him suspiciously. If the code names for Marsh and Martinez were *M&M*, they had to have a cozy relationship with Mr. Big Stuff.

He squinted back at me. "Okay, I lied to you a moment ago, when I told you they were a couple of cowards," he said. "That wasn't exactly the truth. I didn't want to tell you at first, but I guess I have no choice. They're wearing wires tonight."

"What?" I was incredulous. "Why?"

"We were gathering information about tonight's victim, TJK," he said. That was the reason he hadn't leveled with me. "It looked like she was threatening to expose them as the unindicted codefendants. We wanted to know how she knew that."

"Did she know they'd turned state's evidence?" I inquired.

"Apparently not," he replied. "If she did, she would have shut up like a clam. But she was like a faucet, threatening to expose M&M if they didn't submit to her plans. She wanted them to buy units in Vauxhall Row."

"Vauxhall Mews," I corrected him.

"Whatever," he replied. "If she had known they were cooperating with us, it would have meant there was a leak in our internal operation. That would have been problematic. So far as we can figure, all she knew was that they were the individuals referenced in the indictment."

While Mr. Big Stuff was talking, I pulled out the piece of paper I had found on the floor and reread it: "Meet me Verily at Midnight up in the attic." Initially, I hadn't assigned any significance to the capital letters. Now I did. VM. Plus, the message was framed by a rectangle with a line extending down on one end. That was supposed to be a flag and flagpole. Whoever wrote that note was saying something about Vauxhall Mews to whomever was the intended recipient of the note.

I tucked the note back in my pocket, scratched my forehead, and thought of something else. "You mean you were sitting in a van outside of this building tonight, listening to everything they were saying, including their conversation with TJK?" I asked.

"Yup," he said without any hesitation. "We're parked less than a block away."

A song started resonating in my mind. It was "Mr. Big Stuff" by Jean Knight, released by Stax Records, and defined by its two-bar, off-beat bass lines: *Mr. Big Stuff, Who do you think you are?* I mean, who did he think he was?

It occurred to me that this could actually work to my advantage. "Did you hear anything that'll help me identify the real killer?" I asked.

"Unfortunately not," he answered. "I wish that had been the case. But you understand our dilemma now, don't you? If you put M&M up on that stage, it could jeopardize our whole operation. Not only is it going to expose them, it'll reveal everything we were doing. As if that isn't bad enough, it'll also wrap them in the middle of a criminal investigation. No one wants that, especially us, you know?"

I thought of melting chocolate on court papers. "Yeah," I said. "I'll drop them as suspects." Then I had a brainstorm. "Do you have their conversations on tape?" I asked.

"They're back in the van," he said. "What are you interested in?"

"The conversation between TJK and M&M, obviously," I said without hesitation. I could care less about their chit-chat with other people throughout the evening. If I could hear their conversation with TJK, I might glean something about her modus operandi, which could prove to be part and parcel to her demise.

"I'll see what I can do," he said.

A Sade song started playing in my mind. "Smooth Operator." It suddenly pushed "Mr. Big Stuff" out of the Top 40.

In case you're wondering, "Smooth Operator" was written by Sade Adu and Ray St. John when they were both members of the band Pride. However, it was recorded after St. John left the group and the band was renamed Sade. "Smooth Operator" was not written about anyone in particular, like, say, "You're So Vain," Carly Simon's signature hit.

The Smooth Operator swiveled around and was headed to the door.

"Not so fast," I said. "Seeing what I can do isn't good enough. Either you get me the tape or I put them on the stand, and I don't give a damn whether they blow their cover or not. Your undercover operation is less important to me than figuring out who's responsible for TJK's murder."

It was evident from his facial expression that I had struck a nerve. It was also evident that he initially had no intention of returning with the tapes. My threat changed his demeanor and his calculus. He had something I wanted, and I knew something that he wanted to keep under wraps:

In other words, the classic ingredients of a quid pro quo.

Speaking of which, a lot of people think that a quid pro quo is a bad thing. Nothing could be further from the truth. I think the quid pro quo — the Latin translation of which is "what for what" — is the grease that lubricates the gears of society.

The current situation is a great example. He wanted to maintain the anonymity of his sources, not because he cared about M&M but because he was safeguarding his investigation and, by extension, his own reputation and future advancement. In turn, I wanted to acquire a better understanding of TJK to help crack my case, and the tapes afforded that opportunity.

"I'll put M&M on the stand if I don't hear back from you in…" I looked at my watch for effect before adding, with emphasis "…15 minutes."

He nodded his head in acknowledgement. He was clearly pissed, but there was nothing he could do about it. "All right," he said. "I'll go back to the surveillance truck and pull the tapes. Give me your email address."

"Perfect," I said. "As soon as that's done, I'll pass on calling them." I gave him my email address and, with that, he was gone. I wasn't sure he would follow through. But, if he didn't, I intended to grill M&M on the stand.

Before we move on, I want to say a word about "You're So Vain" in case you're wondering about the subject of that song.

Initially, people believed it referred to Mick Jagger of The Rolling Stones, who sings backup on the tune. Carly Simon disabused fans of that connection, which was replaced by speculation that the subject was Cat Stevens (Yusuf Islam, born Steven Demetre Georgiou), David Bowie, David Cassidy or James Taylor, who was married to Simon just before she wrote the song.

Simon shared that the subject's name contained the letters A, E, and R, resulting in further speculation that it referred to musician Daniel Kent Armstrong, whose name contains those letters. About ten years ago, she admitted that Warren Beatty is the subject of one of the verses.

Talk about mysteries! It's been 50 years since that song was written and people are still trying to figure it out. And I'm feeling pressure to solve a murder in one night!

Chapter Twenty-four — Teller Me the Truth

I returned to the ballroom. Murmurs abounded and a fair amount of grousing was in the air as well. A clean-up operation was needed, I determined. Everyone was anxious for the show to get underway. Suddenly, I couldn't find my outline. It felt like I had lost the net beneath the high wire.

What to do? I lowered my head and rubbed the back of my neck. I took two steps in one direction, pivoted, and two steps back. I was in a quandary as to where to resume or, more to the point, where to start.

Then I remembered the lines from "Alice in Wonderland," that marvelous book by Lewis Carroll.

The White Rabbit put on his spectacles. "Where shall I begin, please your Majesty?" he asked. "Begin at the beginning," the King said gravely, "and go on till you come to the end: Then stop."

No better advice has ever been rendered in any class about courtroom advocacy. I didn't know how the case would evolve, did I? So why not start at the beginning? For me, that was the conversation I'd overheard between Mari Teller and TJK. If I could pull that thread, maybe it would keep unraveling.

I went to Martinez and Marsh, who were standing around, unsure what to do, and told them they could take a seat in the audience for now.

"I call Mari Teller to the stand!" I announced loudly. A buzz went around the room. Why the change in witnesses?

She approached with her snifter, which she placed on the floor by her chair as she sat down. She studied the audience. The murmuring ceased. People resumed their seats. The room hushed.

I wasted no time getting down to business. "You didn't like TJK, did you?" I asked.

"That's not true," she replied. "We have a lot of personal and professional dealings." She paused. Then she corrected herself and said, "We had a lot of personal and professional dealings."

The change from present to past tense was significant. Everyone noted it. A page had been turned.

"We didn't always get along, but who does in business?" Teller continued. "Sure, there were spats between us. Some of them were ugly. But we ironed them out. After all, we both have a vested interest in the success of our city."

"Then why did you threaten her tonight?" I asked. Before she could deny it, I added: "You were afraid she was angling to remove you from your position on the planning commission, weren't you? She'd been spreading rumors that you had a conflict of interest in opposing development of a parcel in the Eisenhower Valley. Isn't that true?"

Teller reached down for her glass and took a large gulp of brandy. "She was a conniving bitch," she said matter-of-factly.

Bravo for her, I thought silently to myself. It was a brilliant tactical maneuver. Rather than disguise your feelings or beat around the bush, come right out and say it. I lecture witnesses to do that all of the time. It lends authenticity to your testimony. You've addressed the elephant in the room. And you haven't admitted to committing any crime.

I already knew she wasn't the one responsible for TJK's death. If she was, she would have been evasive or equivocal. I could have ended there but I wanted to try to pull strings and see whether something was going to materialize.

"How was she conniving?" I asked.

"She didn't want me prying into her dealings with Vauxhall Mews," answered Teller. "I'm not sure what the big secret was, but she was deathly afraid of anyone looking too closely at her goings-on. So she found something about me that was embarrassing and threatened to expose me if I didn't butt out of her business."

"What was it?" I asked. It was the question that interested

everyone in the room.

Teller drained the remaining brandy. She sighed. "I don't know," she said. "Nothing. I don't want to talk about it. It was personal."

I stared at her insistently.

"Okay," she said, the brandy seeming to have loosened her up. "I helped my nephew with some city business." She placed the glass back on the floor by her chair.

"Influence peddling," I said.

"No," she replied. Then, "Yes." Finally, "I don't know. I'm too nervous to remember the details right now, but it wasn't that bad. Nonetheless, TJK found out and sunk her fangs into it."

I asked a series of questions to gain familiarity with the project. It involved a wastewater project awarded to Laramie Construction Co. As Teller spoke, Mai tapped on her computer like a court reporter, only she was actually doing research as we spoke.

It didn't take long for Mai to feed me the details via email.

"Your nephew's construction company received a $20 million contract to replace storm sewers along Hooff Run," I said, reading from my phone. "There's no record of a competitive bid process for the contract. Can you explain that?"

It was apparent to me that we were talking about an under-the-table transaction to assist a struggling family business. Furthermore, $20 million was a lot of money. No surprise that Teller was too nervous to remember the details.

"My nephew has unique expertise in a niche market," she explained, struggling to put a bow on her conflict of interest. "Sole source contracts are good for the city. And it helped a small local business, which puts money in our tax coffers."

Her explanation was met with skepticism from the assemblage, which responded with a series of "hmms" and "hahs."

"I think you're describing a criminal offense," I replied unsympathetically. "Was that why you lured her into one of the rooms upstairs and stabbed her to death?"

This being a somewhat informal affair, someone walked up with a fresh snifter filled with brandy, placed it by the chair, and removed the empty glass. Teller looked down at it. She didn't raise the glass to her lips. Instead, she licked her lips. Her eyes closed into slits. A painful expression flicked across her face. She looked vacantly into the distance.

Silence enveloped the room. Rain lashed against the glass windows. Wind rattled the panes. Thunder crackled. For an instant, the lights flickered.

"I was the victim of TJK's extortion," Teller explained. "I don't how she found out, but she did. She pushed me around, demeaned me and sidelined me. I tried to fight back. But I couldn't do it effectively and she knew it. I was putty in her hands."

She availed herself of the brandy. After a reflective sip, she said, "She was a bully. She scared me. And she brought out the worst in me." She replaced the glass on the floor.

Teller bowed her head in disgrace. Her persona imploded. I could see her submitting her resignation from the voluntary commission to City Hall on Monday. Then she'd move to Fort Lauderdale or Scarsdale and retire in anonymity.

"I certainly had the motive and the desire, but I didn't have the opportunity." She began sobbing as the impact of her revelation hit her head-on. "I never left this floor, and I didn't even go to the bathroom. It wasn't me."

Like I said earlier, you didn't have to be Perry Mason to know she was telling the truth. I told her she could step down.

As she was getting up from the stand, Mo Katz appeared in the doorway. He cocked his head and signaled for me to see him outside. I announced a short recess and stepped outside. "Come on upstairs," he said. "I think you should see this."

Chapter Twenty-five — It's All the Rage

Even though Katz had given me a quick outline of the murder scene, I didn't expect what I saw—and felt.

TJK was sprawled on the floor, each hand and leg pointed to a different direction like a broken doll. An ice hook had been driven deep into her flesh and was sticking out from her neck. Blood was pooled around her head; the tips of her black hair were drenched in it. A spray of her blood spattered the wall next to the body.

Neither a legal mind nor a copper's skill was needed to see the invisible emotion that permeated the murder room: sheer, unadulterated, blind rage.

You don't just pick up an ice hook, raise it over your head, and plunge it deep into the neck of another human being on a whim.

You need two things.

The first is a combustible substance, and I'm not talking about nitroglycerin or anything like that. I'm referring to the thing that seethes inside of a person. Hate. Anger. Loathing. Detestation. Abhorrence. Choose any word or combination of words you like. They all stand for the same proposition: evil.

The second is a fuse. Again, I'm not talking about the kind you light with a match. I'm talking about a word, gesture, threat, or exhortation that ignites the combustible substance inside of a person.

This crime was vicious, ferocious, and unhinged. The scene was a manifestation of a simmering hatred that erupted in full force. Whoever killed TJK detested her. And she had said or done something tonight that allowed that anger and hate to blow up.

Katz understood it when he saw the body. That's why he requested I come upstairs. He wanted me to see it with my own eyes. He wanted me to feel it. This was the most important clue in the case, lying right here on the floor in front of me.

I didn't need forensics to solve this crime. All I needed was to figure out the origin of the rage and the words or actions that ignited the rage. That would take me to the murderer.

"Mo," I said. "This changes everything."

He nodded affirmatively.

"I've got to change my approach," I acknowledged. "This is deep. We're dealing with some kind of a psycho." As I spoke, I was already thinking how to prod someone into sharing the secret that precipitated the rage that led to a savage murder in the square room with the yellow lightbulb.

"Keep it simple," he said. "Be direct. And be true."

"Okay," I said. It was sound advice. I knew I'd heard it earlier tonight, but it seemed too long ago to remember when and where.

I also noticed something in his eyes. Instinctively, I knew what it was. I hadn't visited the scene as the first order of business. He had to call me up here. It's a precept that I know he preaches to his prosecutors. *Always go to the scene of the crime. Familiarize yourself with it. You'll learn things simply by looking around. The case will crystallize for you.*

I thanked him and turned to go downstairs. As I do so, however, let me say a word about the ice hook.

The hook had been plunged so deeply into TJK's neck that only the handle was visible. Other ice hooks in the room were laid out on a shelf like dentists' tools. For those of you unfamiliar with an old-fashioned ice hook, let me tell you, it is pretty fearsome. Though there are different types, this one appeared to be an iron, J-shaped hook, maybe 18 inches in length, with a clunky wooden handle at the end. Judging from the others on display, the tip of the hook was probably a very sharp, nasty thing. Imagine a fish hook on steroids. I tried not to look too closely. Despite the fact that the murder scene was horrific, I couldn't help but imagine the weapon as resembling the iron hook worn by Captain James Hook after Peter Pan cut off his hand. I almost mentioned it on the previous page, but refrained from doing so because it would have destroyed the scene.

Peter Pan was written by J.M. Barrie. The pirate Captain Hook is a classic character in children's literature. On a more sinister note, he is to Peter Pan as Dr. Moriarty is to Sherlock Holmes, i.e., the quintessential archenemy. As Barrie wrote of Hook:

His eyes were the blue of the forget-me-not, and of a profound melancholy, save when he was plunging his hook into you, at which time two red spots appeared in them and lit them up horribly. In manner, something of the great seigneur still clung to him, so that he even ripped you up with an air, and I have been told he was a raconteur of repute.

I wondered if there was a sign here. Was my villain going to be revealed by showing red in his or her eyes? Probably not. I certainly hoped not. Furthermore, the murderer tonight was nothing like a *raconteur of repute*. He or she had hidden among the crowd, seeking anonymity for the horrid crime that had been committed.

You know, a gun is supposed to be kept in a safe place or locked box at all times. I think the same requirement should hold for hammers, axes, saws, screwdrivers, even nails, when you think about it. These lethal weapons are oftentimes left lying around waiting to be a coconspirator in someone's crime.

Not that the hook stuck in TJK was left recklessly on a kitchen or dining room table. Quite the contrary. It was tucked away in a museum's tiny storeroom with DO NOT ENTER on the door.

A hundred years ago, that hook most assuredly had been used to drag blocks of ice into the cellar where it provided a primitive form of refrigeration for meat, butter, milk, and, yes, beer. Now that I think about it, I once recall my grandfather telling me about his chasing after the ice truck down Fairview Avenue in Chicopee.

I wondered what, if any, negative vibes inhabited the ironsmith who pounded that hook into shape on an anvil. Was there a premonition of things to come? Was the fact that the hook would be a murder weapon one day in the far-off future be even remotely foreseeable to its creator?

As I returned to the ballroom, I also reflected on what I knew at this point in time. You could say I didn't have much, which would be a true statement. Yet a pattern was emerging. Fact: TJK extorted Mari Teller. Questions: Did she do the same to others? If so, did it involve some of the things I'd discovered about people tonight? If that was the case, maybe there was more than one murderer, like in an Agatha Christie novel.

I noticed the rain was still lashing against the windows. A somberness had descended over the crowd in the ballroom. They sensed a murderer in their midst. They wanted me to smoke out the villain.

I called my next witness.

Chapter Twenty-six — I Feel Sorry for You

I took a calculated gamble by calling Katlin Ash Brook to take the stand.

I knew that TJK's killer had acted in a fit of rage that had been building for a time. I'd heard Luis Aquila tell Ash Brook that the *bitch* had *squeezed* him and that he wasn't going to put up with the humiliation that Ash Brook and Siri Deng had suffered.

Yes, Aquila was a more likely suspect because he signaled his intent to put an end to TJK's tactics. Yet Ash Brook was a better witness from whom to extract information, or at least that's what I concluded. After all, the bitch had to be TJK.

"Your relationship with the deceased has been tempestuous," I began. "It involved a real estate transaction, didn't it? What can you tell us about what happened between the two of you in connection with Vauxhall Mews?"

She gasped.

Without revealing my reaction, I secretly rejoiced. My question was based entirely upon conjecture. I had no intel that the two women were involved in a real estate transaction. Yet, if I was pulling the threads that were beginning to reveal themselves to me and to the assemblage, it was a sensible path to pursue.

"Well," I said. "We're waiting for your explanation."

"I wanted exclusive rights to market certain properties at Vauxhall Mews," said Ash Brook. "I approached some bankers. TJK alleged some sort of impropriety on my part and threatened to take me down if I tried to hone in on something that she considered her personal domain.

"I hadn't done anything wrong," she continued. "No one has exclusive rights to anything anymore. By the same token, even the hint of scandal can have a devastating effect upon one's personal or professional career. I had a Hobson's choice: Either refrain from doing something perfectly legal, namely to market the properties, or suffer some undeserved recrimination that could threaten my livelihood."

I tried to read between the lines. She really didn't make a lot of sense. She was speaking in some kind of vague generalities. And what Hobson's choice did she really face?

It sounded to me as though Ash Brook offered to pay someone in exchange for being able to market some of the units at Vauxhall Mews. TJK apparently found out about it and threatened Ash Brook that if she didn't walk away she'd face exposure for violating professional ethics.

"Let me get this straight," I said. A murmur went up in the crowd. We were all a little in the dark, or so it seemed. "You sought to win exclusive rights to market the properties at Vauxhall Mews. Your methods were, let us say, unconventional. If, say, law enforcement found out about it, you'd be subject to civil penalties and probably criminal prosecution. So you needed to keep it hush-hush."

She hung her head. "I'm not proud of it. I was desperate. My sales were falling during the most lucrative period of real estate sales during the pandemic. Everyone was beating my numbers. I used to be the premier agent in Old Town. I had to do something."

"But why murder?" I asked.

"I didn't murder TJK," Ash Brook answered. "I was prepared to pay her, if need be, to get in on the action. If she would have taken it, I would be okay. Otherwise, I would have walked away from the entire situation."

I felt sorry for her, just as I'd felt sorry for Mari Teller. Both of them were good people, I guess. They just found themselves in untenable situations. In Teller's case, it was about helping a family member. In Ash Brook's case, it was about economic survival.

I've prosecuted a lot of people who break the law to survive. This is mostly white-collar stuff. If they turn to criminality to preserve status — to maintain a lavish lifestyle or to perpetuate some myth about themselves — I've got no sympathy. But if they've fallen on

130

hard times and simply try to make ends meet until the next gravy train rolls in, I'll be honest and tell you that I feel bad for them. It's not a lot different from the bum who steals a Twinkie from the 7-11. White collar, blue collar, no collar. It's only a matter of scale.

It doesn't mean it's right, but it does make it human. Ok, go ahead. Call me a bleeding-heart liberal! Maybe that's what I am at my core, which would be ironic because I'm a badass prosecutor. But, after all, we are all a sum of our contradictions. I think Friedrich Nietzsche said that.

At any rate, Ash Brook did not strike me as the murderer. I'd seen the victim. The rage that erupted in that room didn't originate over the threatened exposure of some under-the-table payment. Plus, Ash Brook was fighting to recapture her dominance as the real estate maven of Old Town. She had too much to lose, in my opinion.

BTW, according to the Merriam-Webster Dictionary, a Hobson's choice is defined as follows:

1. an apparently free choice when there is no real alternative. 2. the necessity of accepting one of two or more equally objectionable alternatives.

I'm not sure Ash Brook used the phrase in the correct context. However, my brain was too scrambled to untangle the riddle. Consuming several Dark 'n Stormy drinks, touring the murder scene, and interviewing suspects had discombobulated my mind. I couldn't process anything else without short-circuiting.

I was ready to conclude my examination. Then, I casually asked a serendipitous question. "Oh, by the way, were you drinking Champagne earlier tonight?" Don't ask me why I asked that question. It must have had something to do with my penchant for identifying people by their drinks and glasses. She'd been drinking Champagne from a flute, or so I recalled.

She scratched her earlobe. "At one point, I was drinking Prosecco," she said. "Zara brought it over to me."

"Thank you," I said.

I wasn't sure who to call next to the stand. My confusion resolved itself, however, when Siri Deng bolted to the stand just as Ash Brook was stepping down.

Chapter Twenty-seven — Deng It

I'm not exaggerating when I say Deng nearly knocked over Ash Brook in his haste. "I need to testify," he shouted. "I must unburden myself before my friends and neighbors."

Now you might think I've never encountered anything like this in the courtroom and, in a literal sense, you're right; nothing like this has ever happened in the middle of a hearing.

But that doesn't mean that suspects don't jockey for position. They do. Whether it's testifying against codefendants or offering evidence of other crimes to obtain a favorable plea bargain, people who are caught in the wringer often seek favorable terms by sharing information with law enforcement.

My point is Deng was either deeply conflicted or extremely clever and cunning. Sometimes, you see, the best way to deflect attention from oneself is to stand under the spotlight. That might sound counterintuitive, but it's true. It's basically damage control squared.

Deng sat down, adjusted his chair, and faced the crowd. "If you read the newspapers," he began, "you might have seen an article in *The Washington Chronicle* alleging that I was involved in certain sexual improprieties." A pall settled over the crowd, which obviously had little, if any, knowledge about the case.

"The article only appeared in the online version of the newspaper and it has since been retracted," he explained. "By retracted, I mean it was removed from the paper's website. Regrettably, some copies of the article are still floating around the internet, but, for the most part, the story has disappeared from the public domain."

I recalled that, from time to time, media outlets revise and remove articles from their websites. A case in point is *The Washington Post* revisiting its coverage of the Steele dossier, the scandalous piece about the alleged escapades of a former president. Something like that never happened in the past. You could retract or correct a story, but you couldn't erase it.

I don't know how you feel about that, but I find it unsettling. It's erasing history.

For example, suppose *Time* magazine wiped away the fact that it named Adolph Hitler "Man of the Year" in 1939. It's a reminder that Hitler was viewed favorably in the years preceding the war. Henry Luce, Joseph P. Kennedy, and Charles Lindbergh are just three names who immediately come to mind as people who were fooled into believing that Hitler was something other than a diabolical monster. That's an important historical footnote, in my opinion.

I just have to say one more thing. I'll be quick. I don't mind the removal of Civil War statues if their presence served to intimidate blacks or to glorify past injustice. I never understood why Route 1 was named Jefferson Davis Highway in honor of a politician who served as president of an insurrection. But I was sad to see the statue of the Civil War soldier removed from the intersection of King and Prince Streets.

Lest we forget, Alexandria was a Confederate city. Slaves were traded at the port. Soldiers mustered on the spot where the statue was removed. Many of them died for an ignoble cause. Somehow, something gets lost when we take down reminders of our past. The worst-case scenario is that we forget the past. And you know what George Santayana said: "Those who cannot remember the past are condemned to repeat it." See *The Life of Reason*, 1905.

Okay, enough of that. Let's return to the matter at hand.

"The story that appeared about me was patently false," Deng said with stark conviction. He paused and drew a deep breath. "My accuser was TJK."

His eyes swept across the room like a camera, pausing to make eye contact with everyone looking at him. It was a device I always use with jurors. If you're telling it straight, look 'em in the eye.

"Somehow, TJK believed I was involved in some dirty dealings," he continued. "I don't know where it originated. I tried to dissuade her of the notion. Rather than reconsider, however, she threatened to expose me to the public. She was able to persuade Tom Mann, back when he was a reporter, long before he became the editor of *The Washington Chronicle.*

"When the story came out, I was devastated," he continued. "If you think it's difficult to straighten things out after you've been the victim of identity theft, you should see what's it's like trying to repair your reputation. Once it's in print, people assume it's the gospel truth."

Deng pulled out his phone, found a website, and read the following: "'Siri Deng, who has staked a massive amount of capital in rDNA vaccine development, has been accused of sexual improprieties with underage girls.'"

That was the same article I'd pulled up earlier in the evening. I had to believe it was the only internet posting that had not been taken down. It remained online like some obstinate creature that clings to you no matter how hard you try to shake free of it. (You can use any word you want for "creature," including, but not limited to cat, dog, child, or lover.)

"This posting is the only reminder of that horrible episode," Deng explained. "The newspaper removed the article from its site after I convinced the editorial department to search for the source of the accusations. I had to prove a negative. It's harder than you think. It's much easier to show someone that something exists than to persuade them that it doesn't.

"The article nearly destroyed my investment efforts in rDNA research, which came at a critical time with the onslaught of the pandemic. Fortunately for me, my patients, and, I suppose, for efforts to combat pathogens, I demonstrated my innocence and was able to move on with my life."

I recalled once reading about Ray Donovan. I'm not talking about the American crime drama by the same name starring Liev Schreiber. I'm talking about Ray Donovan, the former secretary of labor in the Reagan administration. He's referenced in Bennie Hill's book.

That Ray Donovan was indicted for fraud and larceny in a construction project allegedly involving the Genovese syndicate. When he was acquitted by a jury in which several of its members stood and applauded the verdict, he famously asked: "Which office do I go to to get my reputation back?"

BTW, the pilot of *Ray Donovan*, the show, broke a viewership record on Showtime when it appeared in 2013. Regardless, I could never get into it. But I wasn't a huge *Sopranos* fan either. Go figure.

As Deng continued to explain his situation, people began muttering and shaking their heads in sympathy. Then came the coup de grâce. Deng said: "TJK wanted money from me. She'd shaken down others by threatening to expose their peccadilloes. She couldn't find anything on me, despite hiring an investigator to dig through my past. When the investigation came up empty-handed, she said she'd fabricate something if I didn't play her game."

Now he turned to me. "Her greed was insatiable," he said. "I'm living testimony to the fact that she resorted to the most ruthless means to get people to do her bidding. For that, I hated her. But I also pitied her. Despite all she did to me — and the energy I expended to restore my reputation — I did not kill her.

"I avoided her. I told others to do the same. Once she set her sights on you, it was only a matter of time before you either succumbed to her power or you were destroyed. There was no middle ground. I am not your killer, Mr. Reese. Your killer is here, no doubt about it…"

Before he could finish his sentence, Buck Robison jumped up and tore out of the room. Everyone was caught by surprise. As he raced down the hall, others followed in pursuit. "There goes the murderer!" someone shouted, which set off a stampede in two directions — after Robison and away from him.

I joined the posse and gave chase, leaving Deng alone on the stand. None of us realized Robison was leading us to the roof of the museum.

Chapter Twenty-eight — Up on the Roof

Robison was up one flight of stairs, then another, and finally a third. The stairs turned into rickety wooden slats. The staircase narrowed. Then, as we turned a corner, we found ourselves at an open door that led to the roof.

Who do you think wrote "Up on The Roof"? Here are three choices: (a) Smokey Robinson, (b) Carole King, or (c) Johnny Mercer. If you selected (b), you would be partially correct.

The song was composed by Carole King and Gerry Goffin. The hit tune was sung by the Drifters, who also performed "Under the Boardwalk." I guess you could say the group had a couple of "up and under" tunes. Actually, you could label them "up, under and on" because the Drifters also had a hit called "On Broadway."

Which reminds me that King and Goffin were two members of a group of writers associated with the Brill Building Sound because their music operations inhabited The Brill Building at 1619 Broadway and the surrounding enclaves. King, of course, also attained fame by recording her own music, along with such other Brill Building Sound legends as Burt Bacharach, Neil Diamond, Paul Simon, and Neil Sedaka.

At any rate, here we were, up on the roof, which was slanted. Smokestacks, pipes, and gables adorned the roofline. The shingles were slick with rain. The pipes faded into the roof and I had to be careful to avoid bumping into them. The rain had abated but the wind howled. My hair was blown askew. I grabbed my coat lapels and wrapped my fingers across my throat like a scarf. To the east, I could see the top of the Ferris wheel at National Harbor on the other side of the Potomac River. To the west, the Masonic Temple shone through the thick, damp air.

Robison was at the far end of the roof. "It wasn't me," he was yelling. "I swear, it wasn't me." He stood up on the edge of the roofline as though he was going to jump off the building. I hoped he wouldn't. If he didn't die on impact, he would most assuredly cripple himself for life.

"Nobody's accusing you," a voice behind me hollered at Robison. I turned. It was Mo Katz. "You're not even a suspect," he said.

Wait a second, I thought. *Of course Buck Robison is a suspect.* I saw him making out with TJK. They were plotting an escape. I couldn't remember the exact details of their conversation, but it was some strange stuff. Truth be told, he was a prime suspect.

Then I realized Katz was probably less concerned about making a false statement to Robison than about having two bodies taken to the morgue tonight, one splayed in an attic room and the other splattered on the sidewalk in front of the building. He had a method.

"That's right," I chimed in. "Just come back downstairs, Buck. There's no reason for you to be alarmed. No one is pointing fingers at you."

Katz walked to the ledge. Robison stepped down. They embraced. Buck started crying on Katz's shoulder. This huge hulk of a man was sobbing like a child. Then they separated and Katz led Robison to the doorway and down the narrow passageway, the rickety steps, and the multiple flights of stairs to the ballroom.

After Robison was seated, Katz walked over to me and said quietly, "I know Buck's a suspect. You've probably got a lot of important questions to ask him. But if you put him on the stand, he's likely to admit guilt when he's innocent or lash out at people.

"I can't guarantee that he's innocent, but I'm asking you as a personal favor to spare him the ignominy of testifying before this group tonight," he continued. "See where it goes. I'll make a couple of calls and try to figure out if there's another angle for you to pursue. Okay?"

"Okay," I said reluctantly.

I wasn't happy about it. He read my face, nodded, and walked away. He was interfering with my investigation. Robison had been kissing the victim. They were planning some kind of getaway. I was surrendering a juicy line of questioning without getting anything in return.

A couple of days later, however, I learned that Robison was more than a star athlete. He was a veteran of the wars in Afghanistan and Iraq and suffered from PTSD. Katz knew it at the time, though I'm not sure how.

I'm just glad I took Katz's advice and never pursued a line of questioning against Robison. Who knows where it would have led? Probably nowhere good. And, by listening to the angels of our better nature, we might have avoided an outburst or reaction that we would have regretted at the end of the day.

I don't always trust my own instincts. In this case, I trusted his instincts, which were spot-on as usual.

Chapter Twenty-nine — ZZ Bottom

After Katz left the room, I looked around. Several people needed another drink, either to warm themselves from the cold that had seeped into the building or to calm their nerves. It had been a night of ups and downs, physically and psychologically. We'd also been on an emotional roller coaster, beginning with a playful *Murder in the Museum* and finding ourselves in the midst of a real one.

BTW, the drinks were now on the house, I heard. Had I not been involved in this investigation, I would have ordered up another Dark 'n Stormy. But that would have to come later.

I called Zara Abadan to the stand. Ever since Ash Brook stepped down, something had stuck with me. What accounted for the change in the drink? You might think it was insignificant, but I didn't. I wasn't sure why. I viewed it as another thread worth pulling to see whether it would unravel the larger mystery of who was responsible for TJK's demise.

"I'm curious," I asked after she was comfortably seated, "where did you get the Prosecco?"

"We went to the other bar," she answered matter-of-factly.

"What other bar?" I asked.

She raised her finger, twirled her hand around a couple of circles, drew a check mark, and answered, "The one next door."

I recalled having seen Flint Silver draw a similar design with his finger as he led Abadan across the room earlier in the night. I had tried to follow them at the time but they disappeared from view.

She continued, "Flint took me to the restaurant. I got Katlin's drink there and brought it over to her."

That was news to me. If there were two buildings connected by a passage that meant there was an additional entrance and exit to the museum. If both bars had served identical drinks, or if Abadan had not procured a different beverage than the ones served at the museum, I never would have learned about the connection between the two buildings. I ran a series of scenarios through my mind. The killer might never have entered the museum tonight. He or she could have slipped in and out without ever being detected.

But before I could say anything, Abadan added, "I'd like to say something." She removed a piece of paper from her purse, opened it, and read as follows:

"I feel sorry for my friend TJK. Before this night is over, her reputation will be dragged through the mud. She will be made to be a monster and, because of that, some will conclude that her fate was deserved. Some may even feel glad that she is gone."

Her eyes welled with tears. She took a sip of her wine. Her hands were shaking. And she continued:

"I want to state clearly and categorically that each of us has faults. None of us is above reproach. And all of us will answer for our misdeeds.

"However, no one deserves to be murdered at the hands of another person for their imperfections, whatever they might be. TJK did not deserve to die. She is the victim of this passion play."

I felt like I was at a funeral and Abadan was giving a eulogy. She struggled to find her composure. Then she concluded, "TJK should be remembered as a warm, loving, and caring person. Whatever her misdeeds, whatever unpleasant facts are exposed tonight, don't lose sight of the fact that her generous nature far outweighed any negative aspects of her life that will be brought to light."

She took a deep breath, folded the paper, and returned it to her purse. Then she looked at me. "Are you finished with me?" she asked.

I'd be lying if I didn't say that I wondered whether her speech was self-serving and intended to distract any attention from her as a suspect. That was probably wrong of me, but it's my nature. When suspects cry and profess their personal feelings for a victim, are they giving us a true expression of their grief or are they simply acting in order to garner sympathy and distance themselves from responsibility?

It's an open question, I think. Yet, in this instance, it put me in a difficult situation. If I continued with my questioning, I would be perceived as unsympathetic and cruel. The better strategy was to stop. I had questions about her movements that evening, but there was another way to get there.

"Yes," I replied. "No further questions. You've been very helpful."

As she stepped down, I said, "I'd like to call Flint Silver at this time."

A sort of hush descended over the room. Everyone remembered the rumors surrounding Flint Silver's complicity in Rodney Caron's death. Despite the fact that Silver had never been formally charged in Caron's death, the matter was never entirely resolved, at least in the court of public opinion.

Now it fell heavily on my mind. Suppose TJK knew something that had never been revealed about Caron's death? What if it wasn't a suicide after all? What if TJK was pressuring Silver the same way she squeezed others?

If the answers to those questions were "Yes," then Silver had a motive to silence her.

Through osmosis, I had sensed the death of Rodney Caron was on the collective mind of the audience. It made sense to begin the questioning on the circumstances surrounding his death. Maybe it would lend clarity to what happened to TJK.

Chapter Thirty — A Silver Sliver

Flint Silver glared at me. He had spent time and money over the past year exploring a run for the governor's mansion. And here he was sitting under a microscope that risked it all. He looked at me as though I bore responsibility for any drop in his popularity rating that might be attributed to tonight's events.

"You recall the death of Rodney Caron in 2020?" I asked. "There have always been rumors about your involvement in his death. Is there any truth to those rumors, Mr. Sliver?"

Oops. Not a Freudian slip exactly, but a slip of the tongue nonetheless.

Was I referring to a sliver of flint? Think about it. Jagged, sharp enough to maim. Deep enough to kill!

While he seemed to catch my mispronunciation of his last name, he didn't correct me. In all probability, most people didn't hear that I'd said sliver instead of Silver. To correct my slip-up would bring unwanted attention to it. So he probably decided to let it slide. That's what a seasoned politician would do, and Silver was well marinated in the stew — or cesspool, depending on your viewpoint — in which politicians swam.

"I'm not even going to honor a question like that with a response," he said.

I persisted. "We know TJK was blackmailing you," I said. Of course, I had no evidence to back up that question. But it made sense, didn't it? If TJK was digging up dirt about others and extorting them in exchange for her silence, it made sense that she had uncovered some unsavory truth surrounding Silver's involvement in Rodney Caron's death.

My phone buzzed. I glanced at it. Mai had just sent an online photo of Rodney Caron's tombstone from a social media site with the following message beneath it: "Unanswered questions will soon be provided about one of the most provocative cases in recent memory."

It had 723 likes.

The website was Douchebags Debunked. It had all kinds of unfavorable commentary, allegations, insinuations, and insults about Donald Trump, Bill and Hillary Clinton, the Bush family, so on and so on. It was a nonpartisan sheet of you know what.

I looked up from the phone and addressed Silver.

"Messages appeared online threatening to expose your role in Caron's death," I said. "You were feeling pressure, particularly since you're planning once again to reenter the world of politics with a run for governor. Did you need to silence your worst critic because she had incriminating information about you?"

My phone buzzed again. Another incoming! I glanced back at the phone.

The new email from Mai consisted of a series of photos of McCutcheon Park. The first was the entrance sign. The second was of a gravel road leading up to a manor house. The third was a body lying on a wooden bridge across a stream somewhere in the park. And the fourth — which appeared to be taken from the manor house looking down toward Fort Hunt Road — was of a red Volvo.

"What kind of car do you drive?" I asked. He looked perplexed. "You drive a red Volvo, don't you?" I expanded the size of that photo on my screen, approached, and showed it to him. "Is this your car?"

Then I informed the audience: "I am showing Mr. Sliver a photo of a red Volvo at the park where Rod Caron's body was found at the time of his purported suicide. My question to him is whether the car in the photo belongs to him."

Ah! I'd done it again! Sliver.

I expected Silver to grab the phone and throw it across the room. To my chagrin, he broke down. The man of stone turned into a piece of putty, the sedimentary cryptocrystalline of paste. It's mushy and splatters when you strike it with the heel of your shoe.

"I fought against Caron, but I would never kill him or anyone," he cried. "It's not in my nature."

I couldn't tell if he was being honest or faking it. It seemed sincere. Still. Maybe he was duplicating the same stunt that Abadan performed a moment ago? Maybe there was a razor blade stuck in the putty.

"Your *nature* has been combative since the day you entered politics," I reminded him and, by extension, everyone in the audience. "The phrase 'politics is a blood sport' was coined to describe people like you. Do you really expect us to be persuaded by this performance?"

He sniffled and stared at me with a ruthless expression. He was faking it. I couldn't let him get away with it. Left to his own devices, he would peel away just enough sympathetic votes to provide himself with cover. Plausible deniability is what it's called, I think. To a man like Silver, everything is political. People aren't people, they're voters. It's a page taken out of modern campaign strategy: If you can't win a particular constituency, just peel away enough votes so that its numbers don't overwhelm you and foreshadow your defeat.

"TJK posted items linking you with Rodney Caron," I pressed. "You told her to take them down. She refused. When you saw her tonight, you revisited the issue. Then, in a fit of anger, you struck at her, isn't that true?"

"Yes and no," he admitted.

I waited for him to explain which part was "yes" and which part was "no."

His eyes darted around the room. He was assessing the mood. He was about to give the equivalent of a political speech.

"Look," he said. "When you step into the public arena, you expect these things to happen. From the moment I heard about Rodney's death, I knew there would be conspiracy theories linking me to his death. I could have written the script, you know."

He put his hands on his lap to demonstrate he was calm and in control of his emotions. "TJK did some dirty things to me, but it was no worse than what I expected her or others to do and, to be honest, it was consistent with what I've done to others.

"So, yes, she was posting accusations against me. She's the one who leaked that my car was at McCutcheon Park on the night of Rod's suicide. And, yes, in politics, you just go for the jugular. Last man or woman standing wins."

He took a deep breath as though he was doing an exercise to relax.

"I'm a rabid animal when it comes to politics," he admitted. "But I'm not one to resort to murder. I'd already been accused of every derogatory item that she was posting about me. It upset me but it didn't drive me into a rage."

He held up his hand and pointed to the crowd. "The killer, who is out there, struck out against TJK because she was threatening to expose something that had not been revealed. It could be any one of you. But it wasn't me. The lies she expressed about me were part of the political landscape long before she came on the scene. She was just one more 'hater.' I loathed her and I pitied her, but I didn't kill her." As he spoke, the finger moved over the crowd like the barrel of a gun. Then he put down his hand and directed his final comments to me.

"I'm immune to threats like the one made by TJK," he concluded. "I laughed in her face. In fact, I threatened to expose her as a shakedown artist, which is what she was, despite the fact that Zara wants us to be kind to her.

"If you want to know the truth, she was more afraid of me than I was of her. She never made me quake in my boots." With that, he stood and walked away.

I could sense frustration building from the crowd in the ballroom. Its faith in me was being questioned. Had it been misplaced? Clearly, I was losing market share. I needed a lifeline. Otherwise, we were going to end the evening without solving the crime.

Chapter Thirty-one — Calling Around

While all this was going on, Katz told me later, he phoned Roscoe Page, an IT guru who operates out of Tyson's Corner. Katz knew that Page's firm was retained from time to time by high-end clients to conduct private investigations. In fact, Henry David McLuhan had once retained Page to investigate an attack on his sister that had factored into the Roaches Run case.

Katz didn't waste any time on niceties. "Have you ever done any work for TJK?" he asked Page.

It was a loaded question. "Good evening to you too, Mo," Page laughed. "Where the hell are you?" Page was at home, watching the rain through floor-to-ceiling windows at his home in McLean. "This is one hell of a storm."

Basically, Page was stalling. He knew where Katz was and what he was doing. Page needed a minute to process the question. Why would the U.S. attorney be interested in whether Page had done any investigative work for TJK?

"Did you?" Katz asked again.

"Well, as much as I appreciate your brightening my evening on an otherwise dismal and dreary night, you know that I can't discuss something like that," Page said. "It would be a breach of client confidentiality—if she was a client, that is."

"Even after they're deceased?" Katz asked. "She's dead, you know," Katz said.

"Yes, I know," Page replied. "David Reese just finished interviewing Flint Silver, according to the information being posted on the internet. I've pretty much gotten a play-by-play courtesy of people who're in the room."

"Talk to me, Roscoe," Katz pleaded. "It's urgent. If she wasn't an actual client, you can share information."

Based on what he'd learned about TJK tonight, Katz was betting Page was too ethical to get involved in her dirty dealings.

He was also operating under the theory that she had reached out to Page since he ran one of the best forensic investigative businesses in the private sector.

Page was silent on the other end of the phone. Though he was reluctant to admit it, the truth was that TJK trafficked in confidences. It was her stock and trade.

Finally, he said, "I never took her on as a client, you're right about that. But she approached me to work for her on several occasions. She wanted the dirt on certain people."

"Like who?" Katz asked.

"She once asked me to acquire information about Bernie Hill and Monica Livingston, who are two of the people at tonight's event, from what I understand," Page said. "Back in the '80s, Hill wrote for one of the weekly magazines and Livingston was newly appointed ambassador to Italy in the Reagan administration. There were rumors that she was really a conduit between Washington, Warsaw, and the Vatican to free Eastern Europe from the yoke of Communist rule."

"You're kidding," Katz said. It sounded to him like something out of a Tom Clancy novel.

"Glasnost, Perestroika, Gorbachev, Solidarity, the attempted assassination of the pope," said Page, adding a few other names and words that Katz didn't recognize. "It was before your time. Livingston was on the periphery of the communications stream."

"What was TJK's interest?" Katz asked.

"TJK kept book," Page explained. "If she could confirm a rumor, she'd leverage it against you somewhere down the line. 'Either do my bidding or I'll blow your cover.' Along those lines."

"What was the connection between Livingston and Hill?"

"Hill broke a series of news stories about U.S.-Soviet relations," said Page. "That was back when 'breaking news' wasn't just a label to attract eyeballs. Hill was one of the hottest reporters in town, along with Tom Mann, Matt Drudge, and others.

"TJK was curious to know if Livingston was Hill's source. If that was true, she could threaten to go public with the information, which would have cut off the pipeline and disadvantaged both of them," he continued. "Like I said, TJK traded in confidences. *Knowledge is power.*"

"That doesn't rise to the level of what I'm seeking," Katz confided. "I'm looking for something that would prove fatal if disclosed."

"You're looking for the motive for murder," Page said. "That being the case, I can't help you. I never accepted her entreaties. I always suspected she was going to blackmail someone somewhere down the line. I wanted nothing to do with it. To be honest, I always assumed it was going to end badly for her."

"Okay," Katz said. He sounded disappointed. The call had taken him to a dead end.

"Call Tom Mann," Page said.

"Why Tommy?"

"At one point, early in his career, he went after her," Page explained. "He was a stringer at the time, a couple of years before he was scooping stories and earning a reputation as a muckraker. Anyway, he did an expose about her. Then it stopped. And the stories were deleted from the newspaper's website. Ask him why. Maybe you'll learn something valuable about her modus operandi."

Katz thanked Page, hung up, and immediately dialed Mann.

"I was half expecting your call," Mann said. "I heard about TJK's murder. Is it true? There's a lot of chatter on social media, but I have no formal confirmation. I'd like to run a story."

"I can confirm it," Katz said.

"For the record?"

"Yup," Katz said. "You can say that you spoke to the U.S. attorney for the Eastern District of Virginia, who was attending an event at the museum."

"OK," Mann said. "Let me add that now." He tapped his keyboard, adding the lead paragraph to an article prepared for online publication.

> Theodosia Jaidah Kessler, a well-known socialite in Old Town Alexandria, was killed tonight during a performance of *Murder in the Museum* at Gadsby's Tavern Museum in Alexandria, according to U.S. Attorney for the Eastern District of Virginia Mo Katz, who attended the affair.

"All right, it's posted," Mann said. He took a breath and sat back in a worn leather recliner. "Thanks, Mo. How can I return the favor?"

"What can you tell me about TJK?"

"For openers, she was dangerous," Mann explained. "She was two people. To those who only knew her on the surface, she was gregarious, fun, and extremely caring. To those who really knew her, she was ruthless and conniving."

"She took advantage of people, based on what I've been told," Katz said.

"It was how she operated," Mann confirmed. "She enlisted forensic experts to investigate peoples' financial situations, and private investigators to look into someone's personal affairs. There's always something, you know. She'd find it and then she'd exploit it."

"You're describing a criminal offense, namely blackmail," Katz said.

"Indeed, I am," answered Mann.

"Why wasn't it ever reported?" Katz asked. "Why didn't anyone ever tell me? Why didn't you, for example?"

Mann laughed. "Isn't it obvious? She was untouchable. If you tried to expose her, you risked being destroyed."

"It's my understanding you did a series of stories on her," Katz said. "Then you stopped. Not only did you stop writing about her, but the existing stories were removed from the paper's website, or so I've been told. That's pretty extraordinary. It sounds like she scared you."

Mann continued laughing. "And I don't scare easy, Mo."

"What happened?" Katz pressed. "What was it about?"

"It was a long time ago," Mann said. "Most people have forgotten. I took down the stories. She threatened to reveal one of my sources. I didn't have a choice."

"I'm not a journalist, but there's got to be more of a story there," Katz replied. "You know I don't break confidences, Tommy. What gives?"

Mann took a deep breath. "I was having an affair with Sophia Silver."

"Flint Silver's wife?" Katz laughed.

"Yeah," Mann replied. "She fed me inside information about her husband, whom she detested. He could never figure out how the stories were making their way into the press. When I started digging into TJK's activities, she, in turn, learned of the affair and threw it in my face."

Katz knew that explanation wasn't the whole truth. He figured Mann only told enough of the truth to feign honesty. It was an effective tactic to repay Katz for the confirmation and to get the U.S. attorney off his back. Katz decided to play along. After all, he was seeking information about TJK. He had no interest in knowing the whole truth behind the decision to erase TJK from the *Chronicle*'s files.

"Who wanted to kill her?" Katz said.

"On the basis of what I just told you, a lot of people at one time or another," Mann said.

"Can you give me names?" Katz asked.

"No can do," Mann answered. "I'd just put my trust in David Reese. From the online reports, he's doing a reasonably credible job. Just tell him to keep digging. Sooner or later he'll strike pay dirt."

Chapter Thirty-two — Luis Luis

Meanwhile, I was floundering. I'd gotten nowhere with Mari Teller, Katlin Ash Brook, Zara Abadan or Flint Silver. Oh, sure, I could re-call them. I could even accuse one of them of being the murderer. But, in my heart of hearts, I knew none of them was responsible for the fate that had befallen TJK.

The next person on my list was Luis Aquila. As I called his name, I thought again of *The Bridge of San Luis Rey*. That story was about people who were fated to traverse a bridge at the moment when it collapsed.

Might the same be true of Luis Aquila? Might it have been his fate to cross paths with TJK on a night when passions ran high, threats were thrown about cavalierly, and a word was spoken or a gesture was made with just enough moxie to ignite a conflagration?

Maybe.

"Earlier tonight, I overheard you tell two of your compatriots that you weren't going to let TJK *squeeze* you anymore," I said. "I assume you weren't referring to an affectionate hug, particularly since you called her a 'bitch.' Do you mind telling us the circumstances under which she was applying pressure to you?"

Aquila's feet were tucked under the chair, one ankle over the other. He was wearing black boots. Suddenly he thrust out his right leg. It hit the snifter that the Good Samaritan had brought to Mari Teller and that had been sitting undetected beside the leg of the chair, at least until now.

The glass flew into the air like a football, then crashed heavily on the floor in front of the first row of seats. Shards of glass flew in all directions and drops of wine splashed those seated in the front row. Screams of "I'm hit!" and "I have glass in my hair!" could be heard, followed by someone hollering, "I'm bleeding!"

Aquila smiled and said, "Oops! Sorry!"

My first thought was *Good thing it's not red wine*. My next thought was *Damn, another interruption.* It took ten minutes to clean up the mess and calm everyone.

"Can you repeat the question?" Aquila asked when we finally resumed, the shards of glass having been swept up from the floor and shaken out of peoples' hair and clothing.

My examination risked becoming anticlimactic or ineffective at the very least, or laughable at worst. The fact that Aquila smiled throughout the question-and-answer session only added to the seemingly ludicrous nature of this prolonged and inconclusive interrogation.

"What brought you here tonight?" I asked, pursuing my *San Luis Rey* connection.

"To see her," he said. "I planned it."

Was he confessing? I wondered. "The murder?" I asked. My voice cracked as I posed the question. "Are you saying your actions against TJK tonight were deliberate and premeditated?"

"And with *malice aforethought*," he added with a laugh. Given the grave looks that suddenly appeared on many faces in the room, he quickly clarified his statement. "Nah, not like that," he smiled. "It wasn't like that at all. I came to warn her to tone it down. She was getting too pushy for her own good. The woman was looking for trouble."

Let me add a clarification of my own. All these words — premeditated, deliberate, and malice aforethought — convey the same thing, namely state of mind at the time of the commission of the crime.

Intent does not have to be planned well in advance of the commission of a crime. It need only exist at the time the crime is committed. For example, in TJK's case, if the defendant — whoever he or she is — says they didn't come to *Murder in the Museum* to kill her, it doesn't vitiate intent.

Got that?

Malice Aforethought is also the title of a 1931 crime novel by

Anthony Berkeley Cox.

The interesting thing about the book is that it used the "inverted detective story" technique where you learn the identity of the murderer in the opening scene. The technique was used very effectively in the *Columbo* television series starring Peter Falk, where the viewer saw the murderer commit the crime and then watched as Lt. Columbo figured it out. In *Malice Aforethought*, Cox tells us the murderer's name in the first sentence.

It would be as if I started this story by writing, "Three hours before Mari Teller murdered TJK, she was drinking a glass of white wine." An opening like that turns the whole story around. Instead of trying to figure it out, you observe how I figure it out.

The "inverted detective story" is not my preferred technique. But, who knows, maybe I'll use it someday.

And, in case you're worried, rest assured that Mari Teller didn't commit the crime. She's a suspect, a Top 12 candidate. If I actually did that now, halfway through the story, you'd be justified in accusing me of using a "perverted detective story" technique and spoiling it for you, particularly after you've endured all of my diversions and side stories.

Speaking of which, I have one more for you. Who directed the first episode of the first season of *Columbo*? Three guesses: (a) Martin Scorsese, (b) Steven Spielberg, or (c) Richard Irving. You'd be correct if you selected (b).

That's actually a trick question. While Spielberg directed the episode "Murder by the Book," there were two earlier pilots — "Prescription: Murder" and "Ransom for a Dead Man" — both directed by Irving. Although technically those shows weren't pilots because *Columbo* was never supposed to be a series. The 90-minute "Prescription: Murder" — written as a stage play and adapted for television by Richard Levinson and William Link — was intended as a television movie-of-the-week but proved wildly popular with viewers.

I'm not sure how many years *Columbo* lasted on television, but Peter Falk rode around the streets of Los Angeles for several years in a beat-up convertible smoking cigars and solving murders. And it wasn't a Volvo. Lt. Columbo drove a '59 Peugeot 403.

I wished I'd be as lucky as the lieutenant tonight as I turned my attention back to Luis Aquila.

"What sort of trouble?" I asked him.

"Just look what happened," Aquila replied. "Someone hooked her like a fish. The reason is simple. She made her business learning the vulnerabilities of her friends. Equipped with that personally sensitive information, she resorted to extortion. It caught up with her. Someone couldn't take it any longer and put an end to it."

"What was your secret?" I asked. Even I was losing interest in the questioning at this point.

"Why do you care?" Aquila suddenly bellowed. "What good is it to you? You pry into our personal affairs. You're a kind of social voyeur. Do you get your kicks out of exposing our foibles? Don't you have enough of your own?

"We aren't the enemy," he continued. "Don't you bloody see that? We're the victims. So quit looking into our personal lives. Look into hers. That's where you'll find your killer. You won't find the killer by looking into my secrets."

For the first time, Aquila's smile was gone. He'd hidden it in his pocket or someplace else. His countenance had changed from pleasant to grim. He glowered at me.

"Leave me out of this," he continued. "I came here for entertainment, not to be your entertainment in solving a murder. I detest everything about tonight, including you."

Suddenly I felt a vibration.

Chapter Thirty-three — Operator, Smooth Operator

My phone was buzzing. I glanced at the incoming email. The Smooth Operator had been true to his word. He sent me an email containing two file folders, inside of which was the entire conversation between TJK and M&M.

I told Aquila he could step down and I announced a brief recess. Then I ducked into one of the small meeting rooms off the hallway, closed the door, and listened to the first file. For purposes of simplicity, Guido Marsh will be M#1 and Sunny Martinez will be M#2.

TJK: "Well, hello! Are you two masquerading under aliases tonight or is that something that's reserved for federal indictments?"

M#1: "I'd appreciate it if you kept your voice down."

M#2: "I'd appreciate it if you just got the hell out of our lives. I mean, just leave us alone. You are such an F-ing bitch!"

TJK: "Follow me, chums."

Noise as the threesome moves across the hall. Noise recedes. Door slams shut.

TJK: "Don't you ever talk to me that way, young lady, or I'll throw so much heat at you you'll burn to a crisp. Do you understand? Now listen, and listen closely, because I don't intend to repeat a single word. I am going to contact all of the major media sources in D.C. and reveal your identities in that indictment unless you act immediately to purchase a unit."

M#1: "You have a lot of gall to…"

TJK: "Don't ever interrupt me, you little pipsqueak. I'm not finished. Do I have your attention? By the end of the week, you will purchase a unit. Understood?"

I was shocked. Even after all I'd heard about "bad" TJK tonight, this was not the tone of voice I'd heard when TJK brought the battered beauty contestant to my office. In fact, it got me wondering whether there was something more to that case. I am going to have to look into this as soon as I finish listening to these tapes.

M#2: "We'll get on it right away."

TJK: "Good. After the unit has been purchased, I will arrange for a management company to visit the unit on a regular basis. They will have an access key. Your insurance payment will be due on the 10th of each month. Further instructions will be forthcoming."

I replayed that portion of the tape and meditated on what I'd heard. It took a while. Now you and I have the same clues, so you might disagree, but here's what I think: TJK pressures people into buying units at Vauxhall Mews. She launders bribes through real estate. She can pull it off without any whiff of illegality. Nobody raises an eyebrow if someone puts down $1 million or more today on a house, sight unseen. So what if the buyer tosses in an extra $250k to sweeten the pot to guarantee the sale? It's SOP in a super-hot real estate market.

Not only was TJK using the façade of legitimate real estate transactions to launder her bribes, but she was demanding a monthly payment for *insurance*. It was just like the mob collecting insurance from the mom and pop stores for "protection." She was a Mafioso.

I finished the first tape and switched to the second one. Everything on those tapes validated the arrangement.

TJK: "After a year, everything is forgiven and forgotten. I'll return the evidence to you. You can burn it or keep it, whatever you want to do. I won't retain any copies. The unit is yours, free and clear. You can do with it as you wish."

M#2: "You're a heartless bitch."

TJK: "Just be glad I'm not demanding that you purchase two units."

I could visualize it. Every inhabitant in each unit of Vauxhall Mews was a victim of TJK's treachery. The development was like a prison. The only difference was that the real criminal was the one holding the keys.

I needed to get back, but I had to look up details about the beauty contestant I represented on the assault and battery against Coates. I had a hunch and I had to scratch it. Here's what I found:

Two weeks after Coates was convicted of the battery in Alexandria, he was fired from his job. He had been vice president of a semiconductor producer responsible for an agreement with South Carolina to build a multibillion-dollar chip-making plant in Columbia, the state capital. Rather than being on the cutting edge of new manufacturing for electric cars, he was now on the street.

It suddenly occurred to me what had happened behind the scenes. TJK had something on Coates. I'll never know what, but that didn't matter now. She told him to buy a unit at Vauxhall Mews, and he refused to accede to her demands. So she used her inside information to destroy him.

She befriended the beauty contestant and persuaded her to press criminal charges. The motivation was not to help the victim. TJK acted out of malice to hurt Coates.

TJK steered the case to me, probably because she knew I'd jump on it and maneuver the case in a way that guaranteed a conviction against Coates. I'm willing to wager that she even had an inside line on the judge, who she knew had been a victim of domestic abuse. Every step of the way, TJK calculated Coates' demise.

I never realized that TJK was totally manipulating me. I'd simply fallen under her spell. I actually aided her in carrying out her devious plot. I was the vehicle through which Coates was prosecuted.

I'm sure she employed similar tactics to destroy anyone else who failed to acquiesce to her demands. I never saw it, and I doubt that countless others did either. All down the line, we were pawns in her game to get rich by extorting people to buy units at Vauxhall Mews.

The bitch squeezed everyone.

Which suddenly reminded me of that line by Marion Barry, the former D.C. mayor who was arrested on drug charges. "The bitch set me up," he said as they busted him and he realized his female companion was a snitch.

The same had to be true about Buck Robison. I'm sure TJK had something on him. Knowing the way she operated, it was probably his PTSD records, which he hid from the public. She had Robison wrapped around her little finger, pretending to be a lover and a coconspirator while playing him for a sap. It was a good thing I listened to Katz and kept Robison off the stand.

I headed back to the ballroom, my head reeling. I suddenly saw everything in a different light. It was like staring at a hologram and suddenly seeing the whole picture. It was all so clear to me.

Chapter Thirty-four — Head Out on the Highway

I ran into Mr. Katz in the hallway. I was feeling deferential toward him again. Out with the Mo; in with the Mr.

"She's been bribing everyone in town," we informed one another at the same time. Great minds think alike! We laughed and then we exchanged notes.

"There's a laundry list of people who despised her," he said.

"If we look at the list of residents at Vauxhall Mews, Mr. Katz, we're going to find that every one of them is a victim of her enterprise," I said.

"Be careful," he cautioned. "You've uncovered her operation, but don't fall into the trap of believing the murderer was necessarily being pressured to buy one of those units. That might be the case, or it might not. Keep an open mind."

I heard him. My epiphany about TJK's true nature could conceivably blind me in my quest to find her murderer.

As anxious as I was to identify the culprit, I felt a deep sense of melancholy. I am incredibly disappointed with TJK. I sort of worshiped the woman. You'll recall I told you that I had to avert my eyes from the glow of her persona. I now know I should have shunned her because she was a ruthless, conniving, wicked, and insidious individual.

Nonetheless, what sort of person could have been so filled with hate and loathing as to grab that ice hook and kill her?

As I prepared to resume my questioning, I searched for a paradigm to direct me. I was reminded of McLuhan's Rhythmic Cycle of Life. I found a napkin, drew a circle, and studied it.

Witnesses were entering the conversation at different points. I thought of a rotary — you know, the kind that exist on many secondary highways, particularly in the Northeast. My familiarity with them dates back to my days working at the bar in Chicopee, Massachusetts.

I began to play with the design, making it more intricate, like a roundabout.

If you don't know, a roundabout is a modern imagining of the rotary. The primary difference is that cars enter rotaries at speeds of around 40 mph, while the entry speed to a roundabout is much lower, around 25 mph.

As I studied the design, I realized the paradigm I'd constructed in my mind didn't amount to a circle at all. It was more like the system to manage traffic at intersections that is ubiquitous throughout Old Town. I am speaking, of course, of the four-way stop sign.

You cannot travel the traffic grid across Old Town without encountering a dozen or more of them. It doesn't matter whether you're traveling across Washington Street or any of the streets running parallel or perpendicular to it through the city. The sole exception is King Street running down from the Masonic Temple to the Potomac River, a stretch of perhaps a mile that is regulated primarily by traffic lights.

It was a moment of revelation.

I'd lived and worked in Old Town for so long that my mind was beginning to operate like the traffic flow system. Stops and starts. Constantly looking to the left and the right to figure out who entered the intersection first and who should proceed next. I was affording too much discretion to the people I was questioning.

As a result, the case was proceeding in fits and starts. I needed a flow.

I needed to get out of the city, so to speak, and onto the highway. Put the pedal to the metal. Just go for it! And so it was that I continued with my examination with a renewed vigor.

Part Three
After 11:00 p.m.

Chapter Thirty-five — One More for the Road

Before I resumed, I decided to get another drink. Nonalcoholic, of course.

I saw Ash Brook and decided to buy her a drink. I hoped there were no hard feelings over tonight's case. I had put several innocent people through the wringer. I'd compelled them to share their secrets and exposed them to accusations that proved to be undeserved.

I tried to imagine if I'd been the one on the receiving end of any of my examinations. I wouldn't be feeling any love toward David Reese.

"A seltzer water and a Prosciutto," I ordered at the bar set up in the hallway.

"This isn't a delicatessen," the bartender commented dryly.

I studied her face. It took me a second to figure it out. "I'm so sorry," I laughed. "I meant Prosecco. I'd like a glass of seltzer water and a glass of Prosecco."

"We don't have any Prosecco," she replied. "Do you want champagne?"

"Did you run out?" I asked.

"No," she replied. "We don't carry it."

That reminded me of my examination of Zara Abadan. I'd failed to follow up with questions about the adjoining bar. And, while I intended to raise the issue with Flint Silver, we ended up on an entirely different track.

I settled for the champagne, thanked the waitress, and approached Ash Brook. "I come bearing a peace offering," I said. "No hard feelings, I hope."

She accepted the flute glass. "No hard feelings," she repeated. "You're only doing your job. You're a good guy. And I hope you and Mai get back together. You make a nice pair."

"Thanks," I said.

"I wish you luck," she said. "It's late. The rain is subsiding.

People are going to want to go home. The clock has become your enemy. Where are you headed next?"

"I'm going to Padington Station," I told her.

Chapter Thirty-six — Padington Station

Just so there's no confusion, I know Paddington Station is spelled with two Ds. I had a stuffed bear with a yellow rain hat, blue coat, and red boots when I was a little kid. You probably did too. In fact, I still have mine somewhere in one of the boxes of childhood memorabilia at my parents' house. No, wait, at least I used to. I wonder if my mom has it in Saratoga or my dad has it in Sarasota. Or could they have thrown it out?

Be that as it may, the title of this chapter is intended as a play on words. I'm closing in on the killer and it appears as though Pad Khan might help lead me there.

Returning to the ballroom, I called out, "Pad Khan," as though I was giving last call to a station.

Khan took the stand.

"Your name isn't Khan, is it?" I asked.

I was on solid ground with this one, thanks to some spot-on work by Mai. I'd shared my suspicions with her about Pad Khan's economics bona fides, including the substitution of Oxford for OxHouse.

She said it wouldn't surprise her if Khan was using an assumed name. "His academic credentials are forged," she said. "What's to prevent him from lying about his name as well? Once people go down the road of misrepresenting themselves, there's no end to it."

Hers was the voice of reason and experience. As a researcher in the U.S. Attorney's Office, she'd come to expect fraud and deceit in every nook and cranny of a criminal case. She'd proved her mettle once again tonight, providing me with a printout of one Pete Caan.

"I'm sorry," said Khan. "Can you repeat the question? Did you say Cann? How are you spelling that?"

What nerve, I thought. "I'm spelling it c-a-a-n," I said. "Like James Caan."

Fun fact: James Caan auditioned for the role of Michael

Corleone in Francis Ford Coppola's masterpiece, *The Godfather*. As everyone knows, he didn't land that spot. It went to Al Pacino. But Caan impressed everyone on the set and was offered the role of Sonny Corleone.

"Yes, I think that's accurate," he said casually, as though I was correcting a minor spelling error.

"So you've been operating under an assumed name for how long?" I asked.

"It's not an assumed name," replied Kahn. "It's pronounced the same way. Someone just spelled it differently one day and it stuck, like a nickname." Like Sonny, for example, I thought. What was Sonny Corleone's real first name and how did he get that nickname? "I should have corrected it, I guess, but I'm too lazy," he added casually.

"So you're not from the Hindu Kush?" I asked. Please don't ask why I said Hindu Kush. I'm totally unfamiliar with geography, even in Northern Virginia, let alone Asia, if, in fact, the Hindu Kush is in Asia.

"Of course not," Khan replied. "I'm from Jersey."

Jersey! This was too much. And the guy showed no remorse. Not even the slightest embarrassment showed on his face. In fact, he chuckled, as though it was a joke.

"TJK knew about your false identity and threatened to expose you, isn't that right?" I asked.

"Not a false identity at all," Khan explained. "People misspell one another's names all the time. I never held myself out to be someone other than myself."

"How about Oxford, for example?" I asked. *Wiggle out of that one, Sonny Caan*, I thought.

"Well, if you look up Pete Caan, you'll see that he was a professor at Oxford once upon a time," Khan said. "I taught a semester there."

At that moment, a rhyme came to me. Don't ask me how or why. It just did.

Pete the cad.
Lives on a lily pad.
Lies by day, lies by night,
Lies on his pad in plain sight.

Weird, I know. I shook it out of my head, or at least I tried to. "You're not on sabbatical from that prestigious university, are you, Cad?" I asked.

Khan laughed. "It's Pad, not Cad." He shook his head regretfully, as though fending off an insult. "No. All of that academic stuff is garbled. I don't know where it comes from. I've never put it on a website or anything like that. I'm not operating under any assumed name or using any false credentials. People just assign all of those labels to me."

"Are you even an economist?"

"I'm an investor," he replied proudly, as though putting $100 a month into the stock market conferred to him a B.A. in Economics, an M.A. in Business Administration, and/or a Ph.D. in quantum physics.

"Got any good stock tips?" I asked facetiously.

It occurred to me that the interview had gotten totally out of hand. Somehow or other, I had succumbed to Khan's con. I thought Pad's train was pulling into the station but it had actually fallen off the rails.

"What was your relationship with TJK?" I asked, switching tracks, so to speak. I was trying desperately to run a respectable line.

"Well," he struggled for a response. "I did recommend a REIT to her," he said, referring to a real estate investment trust. That seemed to remind him of something. "In fact, I was trying to interest her in a SPAC, you know, a special purpose acquisition company."

He stopped replying to me and started to address the audience. "A SPAC is also known as a 'blank check company.' It's created for the sole purpose of raising money through an IPO — an initial public offering — to buy or merge with an existing company."

I had to hand it to him. People love acronyms just like jurors love forensic evidence, or at least used to love forensics until a bevy of lab technicians started getting indicted all around the country for manipulating data and forging results.

"SPACs have been around forever," he continued. "Although they're wildly popular these days, some people still think there's something nefarious about them. Nothing could be further from the truth. SPACs are a great way to raise capital and get a product, or an idea, to market.

"SPACs are bespoke within the investing community, I guess," he added as an afterthought.

Bespoke. There's a word you don't hear too often, I reflected. Pretty sophisticated, isn't he? Classy, even, I thought. Wait a minute! What was he doing? Or, more to the point, what was I allowing him to do? He had effectively grabbed the proverbial microphone from me. He'd done it so effortlessly that no one seemed to notice. No one, that is, except me. And I wasn't going to allow it. For the first time, I was anxious to get someone *off* the stand.

"Thanks, Pad, or Pete," I said. "That's all. No more questions. You can go now." My words came out too fast, as though they were being swept by a whisk broom.

"Are you sure?" he asked slowly in a way that meant *Not So Fast!* "You've imputed my reputation, insulted my integrity, and called my credentials into doubt. I'd like to restore my reputation to this esteemed group, if I could, before stepping down, provided you don't mind."

Murmurs floated through the crowd, suggesting that the audience sided with him. They were probably angry with me anyway. Perhaps Ash Brook didn't hold a grudge, but I'm sure other witnesses were not as forgiving. And many of the people in this crowd were friends with the witnesses. Reputations had been sullied. Maybe this was the time to restore some of broken pieces to their original state, if that was possible.

Khan leaned forward in his chair and removed a wallet from his trouser pocket. He took a Virginia driver's license out of one of the pouches that contained bank and credit cards. He handed it to me. "If you look, you'll see the name Pete Caan on my license," he said. "The same is true for my Virginia Voter Registration Card, which is in here somewhere." He dug through his wallet as he spoke, like an absent-minded professor (of economics).

"What is that supposed to prove?" I asked.

"That it was never my intention to deceive anyone," he said humbly. "I have nothing to hide. I wasn't afraid of TJK for any reason. I was trying to help the old girl by suggesting she create a SPAC for that Vauxhall Mews thing."

Vauxhall Mews. There it was again. Maybe it was a good thing that he had resisted stepping down from the witness box. "What can you tell us about the real estate development?" I asked.

He looked at me coyly. "Nothing," he said. "You're barking up the wrong tree, David," he said. "The rain is subsiding. Go outside and get a breath of fresh air."

Khan turned to the audience. "I do have some stock picks," he said. Everyone perked up. "Companies that produce batteries for electric cars are going to be huge in the new economy," he explained. "I'm putting my money into the auto manufacturers and chip makers. There's plenty of money to be made." Then he began rattling off the names of companies.

Chapter Thirty-seven — Goin' Down, Down, Down

I felt totally demoralized. My latest examination had morphed into an economics lecture provided by the witness to an eager audience. Tonight, my lineup had run up, walked off, or been scratched. If this were a baseball game, I was 0 for 9.

I felt something burning on the side of my neck. I glanced at Katz, who was staring at me. In his eyes, I didn't see defeat. I saw something else.

His eyes seemed to be telling me that, while I might not be the best prosecutor in the world, I was a good one. I possessed reasonably good instincts. I was on the right trail. And, yes, I had it in me to solve this case.

I needed a fresh start, to begin at ground zero.

As if commanded by an uncontrollable force, I left the room, went downstairs and through the front door, and stepped outside onto the sidewalk. The rain had stopped. The streetlamps reflected their light in huge puddles everywhere. A cold, fresh breeze swept around me. Water roared along the curbs and into the sewers at a frightening pace, creating a great whooshing sound as though I was standing next to Niagara Falls.

I found myself directed across the street.

Once on the opposite sidewalk, I turned and looked at the building, which is really two buildings joined at the hip like Conjoined twins. A yellow light shone in the upstairs window where the murder had been committed. I imagined the murder scene, with the assailant raising the ice hook and forcefully directing it at TJK.

I noticed something near the entrance to the tavern. It resembled a well or the entrance to the underground Metro.

At first, I disregarded it. But something wouldn't allow me to be dismissive. Something, or someone, wanted me to investigate that cavernous hole located next to the two connected buildings.

It seemed as though someone grabbed me by the lapels and

pulled me toward the hole. I felt I was somehow lifted over the stream running down along the curb. I found myself in front of the cavern. A series of steps led down to a pit. The steps formed a spiral, like the turn of a screw. I flowed down the steps and stopped in front of a large glass exhibit.

The cavernous world into which I plunged was dark and uninviting. Then suddenly lights turned on. I looked through the glass deep down into a pit.

It was an ice cellar.

Beside the large window, a plaque was mounted on the wall. It informed me that I was looking at an old ice house that serviced the tavern back when horse-drawn carts and wagons roamed the cobblestone streets of Old Town. Blocks of ice were lowered down a chute into the hole to cool and preserve food and beverages.

The exhibit's lights flickered. I looked into the ice house. Then I saw something. I pressed my face against the glass to better inspect the item that had captured my interest.

Before I continue, let me digress for a brief instant.

Back in 2017, a similar thing happened. I was riding my bike at dusk along the G.W. Parkway on Halloween when I stopped at Daingerfield Island and saw something floating in the Potomac River. I squinted repeatedly, trying to convince myself I wasn't seeing a body. But I was. I called 911.

When the body was retrieved from the water, a photo slipped from the locket around the victim's neck and landed in the grass. I picked it up, showed it to Mai, and then we handed it over to Mo Katz. It was the clue that unlocked the Daingerfield Island case. It was also the beginning of our relationship with Katz, which has been a life-changing experience.

Now back to the here and now.

The lights in the ice house flickered again. The item glowed. I'd detected the outline of an ice pick. I squinted and looked closer. I could see red on the tip of the blade. It wasn't frosting.

Looking up at the window lit by the yellow light, I envisioned the crime. TJK and another party stepped into that room. They were carrying drinks, which were placed on a table. Then a heated argument ensued. The room was filled with sharp objects, including cutlery, ice picks, and ice hooks. One of them grabbed a pick to menace the other. They fought, one of them trying to release the pick from the grip of the other.

In the struggle, the ice pick cut one of them. Perhaps it was the murderer. I didn't recall seeing other stab wounds on TJK. If that was the case, the murderer's DNA was on the tip of the blade. Even if it was TJK's blood, the other party's fingerprints were probably on the pick.

At some point, the murderer grabbed an ice hook from the shelf and thrust it at TJK.

All the while, I felt the presence of someone beside me. It was the force that had pushed me out of the ballroom, pulled me across the street by my lapels, forced me down the steps, and planted me in front of the glass window overlooking the ice house.

Was it *The Female Stranger*? Had she compelled me to find a clue to the murderer's identity? Was Theodosia looking out for her namesake?

I don't have answers for any of these questions. Nor do I expect you to believe me when I say I was directed by a foreign influence. And, by foreign influence, I don't mean some Russian agent in a trench coat wearing sunglasses and black leather gloves, and smoking a cigarette. I mean a *supernatural* being.

I will only say that I am providing you with the most honest recitation as possible based upon my recollection of the events of that night.

I turned and raced back to the museum. In a flash, I was through the door and out of the rain. I was about to run up the stairs and into the ballroom.

Wait a minute! Where was I?

I was totally disoriented. Then it occurred to me that I had run up a flight of stairs to get into the building. There hadn't been a staircase when I entered the museum earlier. I had walked into the building at street level.

I wasn't in the museum. I was in a bar. I realized I was in the wrong place. Instead of entering the door off of Royal Street, I had entered from Cameron Street.

I was prepared to go back outside, around the corner, and enter through the correct door when I had a thought.

I went up to the bartender and asked, "Can I get to the museum without going outside?"

"Well, technically you can, but I don't recommend it," she said.

This literally opened a new door into the inquiry.

After I explained that I was doing an investigation, the bartender, whose name was Samantha James, told me how to get to the museum from the tavern. She directed me around a corner, up a rickety back staircase, down a poorly lit corridor, and through a door that led to the museum's attic. It occurred to me that this had to be the route along which Flint Silver led Zara Abadan to get a drink for Ash Brook.

A police officer was stationed at the door joining the buildings. We knew one another, and with his acquiescence I moved down the hall.

The door of the room next to the murder room was ajar. I peered inside. I saw a hurricane glass sitting on a table next to a chair. I stepped inside the room and looked around. Then I proceeded to the murder room, where another officer stood sentry. I glanced in and saw that plastic sheeting was draped over TJK's body. I didn't lift the sheet to examine the body for cuts. I'd leave that to the coroner.

Then I headed to the staircase, where a third officer allowed me passage down the stairs to the main hall. I looked around there too, reimagining the vision I'd had outside.

I found Mo Katz in the ballroom and pulled him into the hallway.

"I've located a second weapon used in the crime," I announced. "It's in the ice house located on the corner. I just saw it!"

I didn't mention anything about Theodosia. I don't want Katz or anyone else to think I'd lost my marbles. That part of the story remains between you and me.

"I know who did it," I said. "The murderer! I know who killer her!" I leaned forward and whispered the name in Mo's ear.

He stepped back and stared at me. *Really?* he asked with his eyes. I shook my head up and down.

"You're sure?" he asked.

"Pretty sure," I replied. It wasn't what he wanted to hear. He was looking for 100 percent certainty. "I need to clear up one detail first," I said. "But once that's out of the way, yes, I'm confident of the murderer's identity."

I also shared my observations and the information provided by the bartender.

"Okay," he said when I finished.

I knew he was going to assemble everyone back in the ballroom.

"Give me five minutes," I said. I ran back upstairs. With the officers' permission, I entered the room adjoining the murder room and, wearing a latex glove that I obtained from one of the officers, I removed the hurricane glass. I also saw a notepad beside it. I took that as well.

I directed one of the officers to go to the ice house and retrieve the ice pick. "Wear latex gloves," I directed him. "Put it in an envelope, initial it, mark it Exhibit A, and place it on the table in the ballroom. Then remain in the room so that we maintain chain of custody."

Then I went through the secret door to the tavern to get Samantha James, the bartender who had told me about the mysterious route to the museum.

Finally, I sought out Mai. "I need you to do some quick research on a suspect," I said. "Please," I added. I lowered my voice and told her the name of the individual in question. "He's 71 years old." I knew that because I had just looked it up. Actually, I had pegged him as being older. "We need to figure out what he was up to in 2010, 1998, and 1986."

"Why?" she asked, curiously. "What's going on?"

"He killed TJK," I explained. "I know how it went down, but I don't know why, at least not yet. Your research will yield some answers as to his modus operandi. It'll help my direct examination. We'll catch him off guard. There have to be similarities between tonight's crime and his previous actions."

"You're employing *The Rhythmic Cycle of Life* theory," she exclaimed excitedly. "That's radical!"

"Indeed," I replied. "If our friend Henry David is correct, there should be clues in his past that we can exploit. He says in his books that actions repeat in people's lives. Maybe we can discover a pattern of criminal activity by our killer."

"I'm on it," she said, grabbing her tablet and rushing to the adjacent room.

Chapter Thirty-eight — Point of Clarification

With the rain stopped, people were preparing to leave, but Katz called everyone back to the ballroom. He said there was new evidence and everyone should hear it. They complied. Then he turned to me to proceed.

"I call Bernie Hill," I said.

Once he was seated in the center of the room, I displayed the glass from which one consumes a Hurricane. I hadn't seen anyone other than Hill drinking a Hurricane.

"I recovered this glass from the room next to the room in which TJK was murdered," I said. "Do you mind telling us what you were doing there?"

I suppose he could have denied being in the room. It was flimsy evidence, to be honest. If I had been in a court of law, my line of inquiry would probably have been denied. After all, I was putting Hill at the scene of a crime based on the fact that a glass similar to the one from which he had been drinking was found in the adjoining room.

If there had been time, we could have dusted the glass for prints. But there was no time. I held my breath as I waited for his answer.

Hill looked around the room. He hunched over in the chair and started moving to and fro on his heels like an old lady knitting in a rocker. His hands were clasped in his lap.

"Yes," he said. "I was there. That's my glass. But I didn't kill TJK."

"I never said you did," I stated quietly. "However, I am asking you what you heard, if anything, while you were there."

Hill pursed his lips. His face wrinkled like a prune. He put his hand under his triple chin and tugged on the flabby skin. His eyes rolled around in their sockets while he mulled my request. He glanced at his shoulders as though he expected to see an angel or a devil ready to whisper instructions in his ear.

"She was talking to someone," he said finally. Everyone in the assemblage leaned forward, as though pulled by a tow. "They were arguing. And I heard her scream." Hill shuddered slightly. "It was frightful."

I had three questions for him. First, why was he there in the first place? Second, why hadn't he told us before? And, third, what exactly did he hear? I took the questions out of sequence, asking the most important first.

"Tell us what you heard," I instructed.

"I heard her talking to someone," he repeated. "I'm not sure whether it was a man or a woman. I never heard the other person. I only heard her."

I didn't believe him then and I don't believe him now. I think he heard the other voice. He could have identified the culprit, but he was afraid. He didn't want to get involved, in my view.

"What did she say?"

"She was threatening someone," Hill replied. "She said she'd reveal the person's true identity. I think she might have had a knife or something at one point, because she said something about pricking someone with something."

He was referring to the ice pick. This confirmed that she was the one who held the item. But right now I was more interested in the other thing he'd said. "Did she mean someone was using an alias?" I asked. "Or was she referring to something else, like sexual identity? What do you think?"

"If I had to guess, she was referring to someone who had changed their name in the past," he replied.

Shades of Pad the Cad. At least that's what everyone thought, I'm sure. That was unfortunate. I was confident that Pad Khan was not the culprit.

Nonetheless, I was intrigued that a change of name was part of the puzzle. I was doubly glad that Mai was doing research on my primary suspect. I was confident she would unearth whatever needed to be dug up from the past.

Oh, by the way, this line of questioning would also be impermissible in a court of law, asking someone to *guess* what someone else meant, that is.

"What did she say exactly?" I asked.

"She said, 'You got away with it then but you're not going to get away with it now, not unless you do what I'm asking you to do,' or something like that," he recalled.

"Anything else?" BTW, this would be admissible as a dying declaration.

"Yes," answered Hill. "She said, 'I've got the evidence in my car.' I distinctly heard her say that."

You'll recall that there was earlier evidence about documents in TJK's car. I never pursued that line of questioning. No matter, I was confident that she was referring to *other* documents.

I then asked, "What were you doing up there in the first place?"

"I needed some space," Hill admitted. "I wanted to write down some notes about things."

"You left your notepad upstairs," I said. "Let's see whether you left a clue behind." Then, placing the pad on the table, I took a pencil and rubbed the graphite against the white paper. It's an old trick that's been employed in many detective stories. There's a name for this technique. I think it's called frottage, from the French verb *frotter*, to rub. It can also have a sexual meaning, but that's not important here.

As I scratched the surface of the paper, I continued my questioning. "Why didn't you come forward with that information earlier?"

"I didn't think it was useful," Hill answered too quickly.

"Is that the only reason?" I raised the paper, blew away the excess graphite, and studied the words that appeared on the surface of the paper. Holding the paper like the ace of hearts in a card game, I asked, "Did it have anything to do with the notes you wrote while sitting alone in that room?"

I read the notes aloud:

> Enough is enough.
> Leave my family alone.
> Do not harass my ex-wife.
> I will take legal action.
> The payments stop now.

"These were your talking points," I said. "To whom were they directed?"

He didn't answer. To put it another way, he answered the question by his silence.

I remembered the piece of paper that I'd picked up in the corner of the hallway just before McLuhan began *Murder in the Museum*. I removed it from my pocket, where I had stuffed it at the time. As you might have guessed, the paper was identical to the sheets in the notepad. And so was the handwriting.

I tore the piece of paper with the graphite smudges from the notebook. I was going to hand the pad to Hill, but I noticed some indentations on the next page as well. I quickly rubbed the marks with the pencil and then tore that page out of the notebook. "Please write your name," I instructed Hill, handing him the pad and pencil. He complied. I took the paper from him and compared the handwriting to the first note. Everything matched: His name, the talking points, and the message were all written in cursive. The L in *Hill* and all the Ls in his note were identical.

"These questions were directed at TJK, weren't they?" I asked, walking away from him and raising the smudged paper. "In fact, you arranged for her to meet you upstairs in the attic at midnight." I held up the message I had stuffed in my pocket. "She came upstairs, as instructed. You intended to confront her."

"Yes, all of that's true," Hill admitted. "Except it didn't turn out as I expected. I went upstairs and prepared to talk to her. She was saying that I had abused my ex-spouse. I had been paying her a king's ransom to prevent her from spreading that around. She was bleeding me dry. It had to stop."

I figured there was a court filing somewhere that alleged spousal abuse, or perhaps Hill's ex had initiated criminal charges against him for assault and battery at some point. Through diligent research, TJK found the information and threatened to go public with it unless she was paid to remain silent.

"Go on," I said.

"I waited for her in the room," he continued. "I had no intention of doing her any harm, I swear."

I felt a volcano about to erupt. I stood back. And I waited.

Hill began shaking. Then a tremor arose from his body, like an epileptic fit. His body raged. "Oh, what am I saying!" he cried. "I did mean to do her harm. She had to stop it." He drew a fist, as though holding a dagger, and banged it into the table. One could almost see a blade in his hand plunging into TJK as he banged repeatedly on the table. "I was prepared to do whatever was necessary to make her stop."

"Including murder?" I asked.

He looked up at me. His face was convulsed. He appeared startled, as though I'd awakened him from a particularly bad dream. He formed a fist with his other hand and placed both of them over his eyes, like a pair of goggles. He heaved a deep breath, then lowered his hands.

"Yes, including murder," he answered, dreamlike. Then he returned to reality. "Except I didn't kill her. There was no opportunity."

"What happened?"

"I was filled with anticipation, wondering if she would come up to the attic, where I was seated, waiting for her," he began, taking us to the scene of the crime.

"I heard her footsteps coming up the stairs," he continued. "The footsteps began to come down the hall toward the room where I awaited her. Then she stopped. I heard another set of shoes coming from a distance. Someone had followed her.

"She must have believed that it was the person who had left the note for her. I never actually handed the note to her, you see. I'd slipped it into her purse when she passed by me earlier in the evening."

I remembered having seen someone stumble into TJK when she retreated into the back room with Robison. Hill had dropped the note into that humongous purse strapped over her shoulder. Later, when she discovered it, there was no way of knowing who had delivered it.

"Go on," I advised.

"It was as though fate intervened," Hill said. He sounded relieved, as though he would have committed murder if another person had not appeared and taken his place, so to speak. "I heard the door to the room next to the one where I was waiting being opened. They both went inside. They argued. I think she pulled out a knife or something. There was a struggle. Then she let out a slight scream, obviously not expecting the person to be so rough.

"I was frightened and alarmed. It also seemed surreal. The exchange between them was almost exactly like the dialogue I envisioned having with her."

"It was similar," I observed, "because that other person was also the victim of TJK's sinister machinations."

"That's correct," Hill acknowledged. "He said the very words that I'd written on that piece of paper. Well, not exactly the same words, but close enough."

I paused. The cat was out of the bag, so to speak. Hill had just acknowledged that it was a man's voice. And, by stating that the exchange was similar to his bullet points, he was acknowledging that he'd overheard both sides of the conversation, despite his earlier statement to the contrary.

"Then what happened?" I asked.

"The other person let out a holler, like he'd been stabbed or something," Hill continued. "Then she let out a loud scream. A really deep scream. Then there was a thud, a body hitting the deck. I surmised she'd been struck."

"Why didn't you run into the next room and render assistance?" I asked. "Or at least run downstairs and alert others to what had happened?"

Of course, I knew the answer. Someone had just committed the act he couldn't quite perform on his own.

"I don't know," he replied sheepishly.

You poor, pathetic man, I said to myself, reminded of a line by Mark Twain: "The more I learn about people, the more I like my dog." Similar phrases have been ascribed to Thomas Carlyle, Madame de Sévigné, and others, from which we can deduce a universal truth: Men are scum. And dogs are pretty cool animals.

"Oh, come on," I scoffed. "Your preferred course of action was to do nothing, isn't that right? You deliberately remained silent. You covered up the crime. And, in so doing, you realized you might be an accessory after the fact."

He looked at me as though I'd just read his mind. It hadn't been that hard, after all. Yet his fear was palpable. He *was* afraid he might be accused of being an accessory. How interesting, I thought.

If truth be told, there was no way he could be charged with a criminal offense, because he hadn't received, relieved, comforted or assisted the offender so as to hinder or prevent apprehension, which are the requisite elements under the criminal code.

But Hill thought he might be an accessory, and that was good enough for me. Good enough, that is, to wrangle a confession out of him.

"You've admitted to us that you heard a man's voice," I said. "And you've all but acknowledged you heard what he said, because you said it was similar to your own talking points. Don't lie to us, Mr. Hill. You know whose voice you heard. Who was it?"

Come, come, I said to myself. Say the name. I already knew it. Yet this would add drama and a sense of certainty at the outset of my next round of questioning. But Hill proved to be a stubborn man.

"No, I can't identify him," Hill said. "I can't be 100 percent sure. And you don't want me to speculate, do you?"

Well, actually, yes, I did. But I couldn't say that; I was stuck. Then I had a crazy thought. People often repeat behaviors they've experienced. Did you know that?

W.H. Auden, in his poem *September 1, 1939*, wrote:

> Those to whom evil is done
> Do evil in return.

To the uneducated, September 1, 1939, was the day the Nazis invaded Poland, triggering World War II, which claimed untold human misery. Auden's words stand for the proposition that victims become perpetrators, which is probably as true a statement as the one that dogs have more redeeming qualities than man. Auden's poem also includes the line, "We must love one another or die," which, I think, are words of wisdom.

Here's what I was thinking: Maybe, just maybe, Hill, immediately after the murder, turned the tables. In plain English, maybe he bribed the murderer. TJK redux, as it were.

I looked down at the words on the second page I had ripped out of the notebook. They read: I know what you did.

I agree with you: Not very original! There is that 1997 movie, *I Know What You Did Last Summer*. However, the statement is short and to the point. It's very effective. I figured Hill slipped the note into the pocket of the murderer, just as he slipped the note into TJK's purse.

Holding up the paper so everyone could see, I said the words out loud: "I know what you did." Then I addressed Hill, "Did you write those words? Don't deny it. It's in your handwriting. So, let me withdraw that question and cut to the chase. To whom did you write those words?"

He pointed his finger, a classic courtroom gesture in any murder mystery. I followed the line of the finger to its destination. I'm not sure others realized who he had identified. Before I proceeded, however, there was something I didn't quite understand.

I recalled Mari Teller to the stand.

Chapter Thirty-nine — Teller Me More

"I'm not going to probe into any of your activities," I said, recognizing full well that she was devastated about the fact that her under-the-table transaction to her nephew had been exposed to the community, casting a proud career in public service into total disrepute.

"What can you tell us about Vauxhall Mews?" I asked. "What was TJK afraid you were going to discover about that development?"

I have to confess that, if I made one mistake the entire night, this was it. I never should have delved further into Vauxhall Mews. For all of the mystery that surrounded it, Vauxhall Mews was a red herring. Even worse, it was a red herring of my own device. I assigned to the development a significance that was totally unnecessary.

Our killer wasn't even remotely connected to Vauxhall Mews. I just didn't know it at that moment. And, as a consequence, I distracted the assemblage — including myself — from a dark truth that was about to emerge before all of our unsuspecting eyes.

"She was using it as her private piggy bank," replied Teller. "She railroaded people into buying units for inflated prices. Most of her transactions were cash on the barrelhead. No financing was provided by commercial banks. The buyers constituted an eclectic class. Several never moved into their residences, which stood unoccupied. It was as though Vauxhall Mews was a straw man, a front for something else."

"TJK used Vauxhall Mews as a sort of dummy corporation to launder the money she extorted from people," I said. "But that wasn't necessarily a reason to kill her."

Teller stepped down.

The reverence in which I held TJK at the beginning of the evening had lifted like a fog off a lake as the morning sun rises above the tree line. Did you like that sentence? I try to avoid coming across as too literary in my writing but I just finished a book by James Lee Burke, *Black Cherry Blues*. He weaves scenery of the Louisiana bayou and Continental Divide into his mysteries. I thought I'd give it a try.

"Maybe our next witness — our final witness — can provide greater detail into the factors that contribute to compelling a person to commit murder," I said, turning to the person to whom Hill's shaking hand had pointed at the conclusion of his testimony.

Chapter Forty — Charles on the Stand

At that very instant, someone who was looking at the weather report on their phone blurted out, "The roads are clear! The rain has stopped! We'll all be able to leave!"

"Please, not so fast!" I insisted. "It's important that we put the cuffs on the culprit responsible for TJK's demise. "I call Michael Charles to the stand!"

Everyone froze.

Muffled laughter swept across the room, as though people were covering their mouths to contain themselves. I may have been ineffective to this point, but that was really par for the course. Only after exhausting every other alternative do I find the right one!

I raised the ice pick and held it over my head like the Sword of Damocles. I was wearing a latex glove. And the pick was in a clear plastic baggie.

People gasped. I twirled it around. "Exhibit A," I said. The officer who retrieved the ice pick from the basement was standing sentry, preserving chain of custody.

That got their attention, although it wasn't actually Exhibit A, which was the ice hook inserted into TJK's now cold body. Boy, you show that to a jury and you've got a captive audience for the duration of the trial.

"Where did you find that?" someone asked from the crowd. People who had started to head to the exit doors returned to their seats. It was as though I had just pulled a rabbit out of a hat. Everyone wanted to see what was coming next. I was not going to disappoint this time.

"It was in the ice house exhibit on the corner outside," I said. "The murderer put it there believing no one would find it. He had no idea it would be visible from the street above. That tells us the murderer was unfamiliar with the building and the fact that there is an ice house display on the street corner outside of the museum.

Like Michael Charles."

Charles stepped forward. He clutched his drink. People surrounded the stage, a veritable theater in the round. He clearly relished the moment. And why wouldn't he? Here he was, the center of attention, the thing he craved the most, like any sociopath, in my opinion.

"You're right, Mr. Reese," Charles said, disparagingly. "I've never been here before. I guess that makes me guilty, as charged."

Everyone snickered.

"I freely admit it's hardly enough to place the murder at your feet," I replied, "but it is only one data point." The statement lingered as I placed the plastic envelope containing the ice pick on a makeshift exhibits table. I continued, "One among many."

I caught the eye of Curtis Santana, who had been lingering near the door to prevent people from leaving. He came over and I passed him a note. He nodded and immediately left the room.

"I notice that your pant legs are wet, Mr. Charles," I observed. "Mind telling us how that happened?"

From the knee down, the khakis that Charles wore were a darker color, clearly the consequence of being soaked by water. Everyone looked at them. His topsiders were also noticeably wet. In fact, a tiny puddle formed at his feet where he was seated.

"I stepped outside to check on the weather a minute ago," he said innocently. He placed his glass next to one of the chair's legs.

"How did you manage to do that?" I asked. "The front door was barred, wasn't it?" He momentarily looked taken aback. "Perhaps you left via some other entranceway?" I asked.

"I just admitted that I was unacquainted with the building," Charles replied. "Therefore, I'm not acquainted with any other entrances or exits. The only one I know is the front door, which is how I left the building. Via the front door!"

"That's a true statement, Mr. Charles, namely that you only come and go by the front door," I said. "But you and I both know there's more than one front door. In fact, sir, there are two front doors. There's the front door that leads into the museum. It's located on Royal Street. And then there's the front door that leads into the tavern. And it's located on Cameron Street. The two buildings are joined at the hip, so to speak, at the corner of Cameron and Royal Streets. Isn't that right?"

"How should I know?" he asked.

I gave Charles high marks for answering a question by asking one of his own. As I previously indicated, I've always found it a successful debating technique. In this case, I was ready for it.

"You stumbled upon it after you murdered TJK. You headed away from the crowd," I said. "You needed to get away. And, much to your amazement, the corridor led you to the adjoining building.

"You went down a flight of stairs and found yourself at the tavern. Then you went out into the rain. You knew that TJK's car was parked next to the building and that it was unlocked. You suspected that certain papers you were seeking were in the car. So you went out the main door and directly to the car, where you conducted a search of her glove compartment, console, and back seat."

At that moment, Santana returned holding a trench coat over one arm and bartender Samantha James' hand wrapped over the other. They reminded me of Rick Blaine (Humphrey Bogart) and Capt. Louis Renault (Claude Rains) walking arm-in-arm in the closing scene on the tarmac in the 1942 masterpiece *Casablanca*, one of the greatest movies of all time, if not *the greatest*.

"That's preposterous," said Charles. "Mere conjecture."

I repeated my previous statement, looking in James's direction as I spoke. "Are you denying that you left the building and went outside to TJK's car?"

"Nothing but conjecture and hyperbole," he cried.

Hyperbole. Really? Conjecture, certainly. But I'm not so sure about hyperbole. Regardless, I went on. "Think carefully, Mr. Charles. Are you sure you didn't go outside?"

"Are you sure?" is code for "You're lying!" It's a great set-up line in the courtroom. And it's one I use with impunity whenever I'm about to lower the boom.

"The bartender at Gadsby's Tavern Restaurant is prepared to testify to the contrary," I continued. "She'll say that she saw you exit and return ten minutes later sopping wet."

Boom!

"Care to revise your story?" I asked.

"What am I, under oath?" he laughed. Nobody else did. They just looked at him grimly. They paid top dollar for tonight's charity event and now it seemed as though they might get their money's worth. No one was checking the time on their phone or wristwatch.

"I might have gone outside for an instant," Charles admitted.

"You *might* have gone outside in the pitch black under a sheet of drenching rain?" I asked, my voice dripping with sarcasm. "You're not sure? Is that it? You can't remember? Perhaps you don't care to remember?

"Most people would remember something like that, you know," I continued. "Wind blowing." I moved my hands from the left to the right, my fingers playfully striking the notes of an imaginary piano. "Rain falling." I raised my hands and then lowered them slowing, my fingers twitching wildly to mimic raindrops. "Which is it, Mr. Charles?"

The gears inside Charles' head were turning so fast that I could practically smell the smoke. He needed some lubrication. But, of course, he didn't drink! I knew what he was thinking. As soon as he admitted to my version of the truth, he was on a downward spiral. He had to stick to the lie.

"No, I don't think I did," Charles said. "I don't think I went outside."

I smiled. Was there any other explanation for the wet trousers and the soggy topsiders? Of course not. Everyone knew that Charles was caught in a lie. It was going to be fun from this point out. I would be sharing the joke with the jury, so to speak.

"Do you remember Samantha James?" I asked, pointing to the bartender.

"No," he said.

"In addition to seeing you leave the tavern, Ms. James remembers serving you a drink," I said.

"I don't think that's possible," Charles said.

Notice, he did not say "No." Just like his answer to the previous question, about leaving the building through the front door of the tavern. He was hedging, keeping his options open. He was lying but his lies were not bold-faced ones. Smart. He was leaving himself some wiggle room.

"Why do you say that?" I asked.

"Because I don't drink," Charles said. "When I socialize, I get a drink and walk around with it all night long. I hold it as a prop, that's all."

I paused. I looked at the leg of his chair and the drink beside it. "What were you walking around with tonight, Mr. Charles?"

He looked at the glass beside the chair. Everyone in the hall glanced at it as well. People in the back rows stood. Necks stretched, eyes strained. The glass was only half full, which was a little incriminating in itself, if you believe his story that he walked around with the glass all night long. Of course, some of it might have spilled over. And maybe he nipped once or twice.

Michael Charles leaned over and picked up the drink. It was a cocktail glass. Ice cubes floated in the glass. A plastic sword stuck out of the top of the glass, piercing a cherry that lay at the bottom.

"This," he said.

"That isn't the drink you've been walking around with all night long, is it?" I asked.

"It is," he said, emphatically. Then, with a little less certainty, he amended, "Or, at least I think so."

Again, the hedge.

"We both know it isn't," I said. "You had red wine in a long-stemmed glass," I said.

"I don't think that's true," replied Charles.

"It is true, Mr. Charles," I said unequivocally. I pulled out my phone. "Just like it's true that you went out the door of the restaurant. And just like you got a drink at the bar from Samantha James. The only difference is that I have evidence in this case. Here's the proof."

I nodded to Mai, who projected her laptop screen image to the large white screen at the front of the room. I had emailed a photo to her as soon as I realized what had transpired. There we were, Michael Charles and me, hugging, with Charles' outstretched arm toasting with a long-stemmed wine glass filled with burgundy wine.

"Is that Cabernet Sauvignon?" I asked. "Le Boucher? Vidure? Sauvignon rouge?"

The "jury" chuckled. I did like saying *sauvignon rouge*. I mean, that could be the title of a murder mystery.

"I don't know," Charles replied, annoyed.

"It's not a cocktail glass, you'll agree with me on that at least," I said.

He equivocated, as I expected. "I don't think so," he murmured.

"Can you explain how it came to be that you started out the evening holding a long-stemmed glass of red wine and ended up with a cocktail glass?" I asked.

"I'm not sure," he replied.

"Ms. James will testify that you procured it a short time ago, and that you asked specifically for a cosmopolitan, the preferred drink of TJK!"

"I did not say it was for TJK!" he responded violently.

Aha!

The audience swooned. He'd admitted to ordering the drink. This was the first admission I'd wrung out of him. Yet, in truth, Samantha James did not tell me that Charles had referenced TJK when he got the drink. I insinuated that. But it was obviously the reason for his choice, whether or not he mentioned it to the bartender.

"Why would I ask the bartender for her favorite drink?" he asked.

Now, under normal circumstances, a witness does not ask questions during a trial. He or she would be admonished by the judge and the question would be disregarded. But, in this case, it played to my advantage so I went with it.

"Because you wanted to create the illusion that she was still alive," I said.

Eyebrows were raised. Gasps were uttered. And several people rubbed their chins.

Between you and me, the idea of establishing a false time of death was something I just pulled out of a hat. I'd watched *Murder on the Orient Express* last week, the 1974 version directed by Sidney Lumet.

By the way, did you know that Lauren Bacall won an Academy Award for best supporting actress for that film? I think she was just the sentimental favorite. Also, fun fact, Bacall was married to both Humphrey Bogart and Jason Robards. I only know that because I look up things in Wikipedia whenever I watch television at home to learn about the show, the actors, and the history surrounding the production.

If anyone deserved an award for that movie, it was Albert Finney as Hercule Poirot. He was nominated but didn't win. And, while we're on the subject, the score was also nominated and also did not win. Good! I never liked the score, to be honest with you. It was lightweight. In fact, I feel it diminished the movie. The music conveyed a sense that the movie was a simple parlor game instead of a complicated crime caper, which it was. The producers should have gotten someone like Jerry Goldsmith, who scored *Chinatown*. With the right music, that movie would have been a classic.

Anyway, assuming you read the book or watched at least one version of *Orient Express*, a timepiece is found belonging to the murder victim, Samuel Ratchett. The timepiece is smashed. It displays a specific moment in time. SPOILER ALERT. It's a ruse to trick Hercule Poirot into believing it's the time the murder was committed, except it's not and he's smart enough to know it.

Oh, no! I wasn't listening to what Charles was saying. I only caught the tail end. "I wanted to do what?" he asked.

"You heard me," I said. "You wanted to create the impression that TJK was alive."

He sat expressionless.

"You killed TJK upstairs sometime around 10:30," I explained. "You knew she drank a cosmopolitan because you placed her drink on a table along with your wine glass when you encountered her upstairs."

Although this was speculation on my part, the parties both held glasses at the moment they encountered one another, at least according to the vision I'd had when I was staring up at the window from the street corner.

"Those two glasses have been taken into custody and will be taken to the forensic lab for testing," I continued. Another lie, but plausible. "I suspect your fingerprints will be on both of them."

Just between us, nothing had been taken into custody, although the glasses lying around probably would be, unless, of course, someone has already picked them up, returned them to the kitchen, and washed them, which was also entirely possible. However, if the glasses were collected and tested for fingerprints, it's highly probable that Charles' fingerprints are on both glasses, assuming, of course, he didn't wipe the fingerprints after stabbing TJK.

"After you killed her, you went to the basement to hide the ice pick." I again held up the plastic bag marked Exhibit A. "As you returned upstairs, you went down the wrong hallway and ended up in the bar. Realizing you were in another part of the building, you exited the tavern and went to her car."

More speculation.

"You searched the inside cabin," I continued. "Then you returned to the bar and ordered a drink for TJK. It was about 10:50. You knew she was lying dead in the upstairs room with an ice hook in her neck. But you had an ironclad excuse because, if questioned, you could say that you were ordering her a drink."

"That's absolutely not true," he said. "Why would I do that? Who cared what time she died? It makes no sense. And, if I'd done that, why aren't I using it as an alibi now?"

He had a point. Had I gone down the wrong rabbit hole? I felt a sudden knot in my stomach.

"You're insinuating a lot of horrible things," said Charles. "I've got a good mind to get up and walk out of here right now. I don't have to sit here and take it."

"You're welcome to leave," I said. "Nobody's holding you. But before you go, would you please remove your jacket so we can see whether you have a stab wound on your arm?"

Chapter Forty-one — Glasses of a Different Sort

He suddenly grabbed his jacket lapels as though his fingers were staples sealing the jacket to the shirt.

"I don't think so," he said.

"Were you nicked by an ice pick, perchance?" I asked.

Realizing his reticence could be an admission, he removed his jacket and displayed his shirt sleeve. "I spilled some red wine on my shirt earlier tonight," he said. "And I inadvertently stumbled into a sharp edge going around a corner."

Since you weren't there, you're not in a position to match his story with what was now in plain view. But judging from the faces of the crowd, nobody bought his explanation.

"And what about the raincoat you wore outside?" I asked. Notice I didn't say "your raincoat" because Michael Charles had brought neither a raincoat nor an umbrella with him when he arrived in Old Town late in the afternoon for the garden tour. You will recall the storm crept in without a warning. Charles' garden tour was cancelled. He was then unexpectedly ushered inside the museum.

I know how Charles is going to respond, and I'm ready with both barrels.

"*What* raincoat?" he asked. Again, this incessant questioning. "I don't think I wore a raincoat tonight." Combined with his penchant for equivocation, the man was frustrating me.

"The raincoat you wore when you went outside to TJK's car," I answered. "This raincoat," I said, accepting the proffered coat from Santana.

"Oh, that raincoat," said Charles sarcastically. "The raincoat you allege I was wearing when you claim I went out in the rain to rummage about in TJK's car. *That* raincoat?"

He stood. Picture the sight, if you can. He's wearing a wrinkled white long-sleeved shirt that has blood on it and is bulging where he wrapped gauze around his wounded forearm. His wrinkled khakis are wet from the knee down. Just looking at him, a word begins to enter your subconscious. It's a six-letter word beginning with the letter G.

Guilty.

"Precisely," I replied.

"I wasn't wearing a raincoat when I came to the event, so I never checked one in the coat room," Charles said. "You can search me for a check stub," he added, standing and pulling out the lining of the pockets of his khakis. He surveyed the crowd, squinting. He touched his breast pocket, as though he was fumbling for a handkerchief. Then he quickly tapped his pants pockets. To a discerning eye, he looked confused.

"Please don't sit," I said. I wanted everyone to get a good look at him. Necks craned. Floorboards made that scraping chalkboard sound as chair legs were pulled forward to enable the people sitting in them to satisfy their curiosity. He fumbled around a little more as though he was blessing himself in search for his wallet and keys.

In case you ever wondered, a courtroom is nothing more than a stage. The attorneys don't recall the past. They create an atmosphere. If the attorneys are really good at their craft, the "reality" created in the courtroom skews the storyline in favor of their client. In this world, exhibits matter. They're visual. And that's particularly important on a stage in which the entire show is performed with words. We don't wear costumes, no powdered wigs and gowns, like barristers. Only exhibits are permitted into the courtroom: murder weapons, photographs, etc.

Having the accused actually wear incriminating evidence is priceless.

"Now you say that the raincoat does not belong to you, which is true," I said. "Yet I submit that this is the item you donned when you ventured out into the rain. First, Ms. James saw you put it on, which you deny. Second, it's wet." I shook it. Water spattered as though a dog had shaken water off its fur coat. "Third, your midsection is dry but your pant legs are wet, probably at the water line where this coat protected you from the elements."

I stopped for an instant. It was for effect.

"And, fourth, you placed something in the pocket of the raincoat." I reached inside and pulled out an item, which I held up for all to see. "Your glasses!" I announced, no pun intended.

I walked up to Charles. This moment always has a certain dramatic effect, and this time was no exception. I sensed some people holding their breath. I regretted not being able to say, "Permission to approach the witness, Your Honor."

I handed the glasses to Charles. He did not take them. Instead, he sat down and stared into space. "I don't think those are my glasses," he said.

"How do you know?" I asked. "You probably can't see them clearly." Everyone laughed. A little levity is always a nice touch in the middle of a grueling examination.

"You do admit that you wear glasses, don't you?" I asked. "And you agree that you wore them here tonight."

"I'm not exactly sure," he replied.

Yet again! Equivocation. I'd seen him wearing glasses. They kept slipping down the bridge of his nose.

"My glasses have a very weak prescription," he explained. "Sometimes I find I don't need them. I'll leave the house without them. I won't return to get them. I can see adequately without them. My eyesight has actually improved over time. The prescription is not as strong as it was, say, ten years ago. In fact, to be honest about it, I wear them primarily for looks. They make me appear more intellectual."

Everyone laughed. I guess it was his turn to add a little levity.

"Try these on," I said.

"I'd rather not," he replied. "I don't know who they belong to, and I'd just as soon not put them on my face, if you don't mind." He stole a smile at me that only the two of us could detect.

"Yes, quite," I said, like a British inspector who'd been stymied in his investigation. The witness thought he was outwitting me. "Well, if it helps," I added, "you're wearing these glasses in the photo that I took earlier of the two of us."

I held up my phone for display since Mai had taken her laptop when she left the room. Even though the crowd couldn't see the image on my phone, they took my word for it and a murmur went around the room. For greater effect, I held my phone right up to Charles' face. He looked aside.

It was all adding up: the cosmopolitan, the bloody shirt, the wound on his arm, the eyeglasses in the pocket of the raincoat. All circumstantial evidence, I admit, but consistent with guilty and seemingly inconsistent with innocence. Enough to convict? Maybe not. I needed the confession.

Just then Mai entered. She was holding some papers. I turned and walked over to receive them. As I did so, I heard Charles clear his throat. Did he suspect what was coming?

Chapter Forty-two — Riddle Me Charles

Mai's research on Michael Charles went back 12 years from tonight's date. If Henry David McLuhan's thesis was correct, the past foretold the future. I glanced at the papers. Wow! I wasn't sure where to begin. Then I remembered the instruction from Lewis Carroll.

"Mr. Charles, the associate dean of the law school where you teach died back in 2010, did he not?" I asked.

"Yes," he said, "but what does that have to do with the murder of TJK?"

What, indeed? "Indulge me," I pleaded.

"I already have, Mr. Reese, to a considerable degree, and I'm getting a little bored with your antics," he said.

I said, "The associate dean was Gifford Winder. He died under mysterious circumstances. There was a question as to whether he had died of natural causes or had been poisoned. No one was ever accused of killing him, but the question lingers to this day.

"Early on, you were a suspect in the murder of Associate Dean Winder. You had actually been in his company on the night of his demise. You were questioned by the Arlington Police Department, though nothing came of it. According to news accounts at the time, you equivocated and obfuscated when asked about your whereabouts at the time of his death."

"What of it?"

"It bears an uncanny resemblance to the current situation, doesn't it?" I asked.

"Not at all," he said. "I think you're reaching for straws." Turning to the crowd, he said, "This bears an uncanny resemblance to the questioning of Flint Silver, which went nowhere." Then, to me, he said, "It was an isolated incident. I was questioned along with everyone else who knew the associate dean. It's standard operating procedure, just as you've been doing tonight. Without much success,

I might add."

I looked again at the articles that Mai had given me. I quickly tried to make sense of them. The topic was a boating accident on the Potomac River in 1998.

I remembered it. Everyone remembered it. It was one of those cases that grabbed the public imagination. It was strange and mysterious, almost surreal, a kind of fictional account playing out in real life.

I must have been in elementary school at the time, but I still recalled the headline: "Old Town Heiress Drowns in Potomac Tragedy." It was a sensational story. In fact, I remember cutting out the articles from *The Washington Chronicle* and creating a scrapbook about the case. It was like a Hardy Boys or Nancy Drew mystery. There were lots of questions about what happened and who was responsible. In fact, now that I think of it, that case was the seed that grew into my interest in criminal law.

It took me a minute to make sense of it. It bore a resemblance to the questioning of Pad Khan, which might have helped me figure it out.

I leaned over and whispered some instructions to Mai, who was again sitting at the table with her laptop open. In a moment, the *Chronicle* article appeared on the large screen at the front of the room.

"Ladies and gentlemen," I said pointing to the screen, "you may find this article very interesting."

The article read:

OLD TOWN HEIRESS DROWNS IN POTOMAC TRAGEDY

By Tom Mann, special correspondent

Lilly Talbot, one of Alexandria's wealthiest women, drowned off Daingerfield Island late last night in a boating accident while sailing with her husband, Marty Chastain.

Talbot, 84, was pulled from the water shortly before 10 p.m. by an Alexandria rescue team. The matter will be investigated by District of Columbia Police.

Chastain, 50, survived.

According to the police report, Chastain radioed for assistance at 9:40 p.m., indicating that his wife had fallen overboard from their sailboat.

Chastain said the couple had been drinking and dancing aboard their boat. According to his statement, she tripped, struck the side of the vessel, and tumbled overboard. She was not wearing a safety vest.

Chastain was taken to Alexandria Hospital, where he remained overnight for observation.

Talbot inherited considerable real estate in Old Town and the District of Columbia from her father, John Talbot, a real estate magnate who sold estates in Northern Virginia to members of the Eisenhower, Kennedy, and Nixon administrations. At one time, a Talbot Real Estate listing was a sign of prestige in the Washington metropolitan area.

Talbot was known as a recluse who seldom ventured out in public. The couple married only a month ago at St. Mary's Catholic Church in Alexandria. It was the first marriage for Talbot; the third for Chastain. Talbot had no children.

After a few minutes, the audience began buzzing in excited conversation.

While the audience read the article, I noticed Charles squinting at the screen, so I handed him the glasses, which he placed on his face. As soon as he did so, he froze, then quickly removed them. "These aren't mine," he said. "The prescription is too strong."

"Too bad," I said. "You're missing a good story."

"Well, let me try to make use of these as best as I can," he said, taking them back. "Just don't assume they're my glasses just because I'm wearing them."

After I was sure he had read the article, I posted a follow-up article by Mann which appeared a couple of days later. It read:

Questions Arise Over Circumstances Surrounding Heiress' Drowning

Questions have emerged about the circumstances under which longtime Alexandria resident and real estate heiress Lilly Talbot drowned last Thursday in a boating accident with her husband, Marty Chastain, on the Potomac River.

According to informed sources, the marks on Talbot's body are inconsistent with the fall reported by Chastain to the police. The autopsy also did not find any water in Talbot's lungs, according to the sources.

Chills came over my body.

The story bore an uncanny resemblance to the Daingerfield Island case in 2017. The victim in that case was killed on land and her body was afterwards dropped in the water. I was the first person to find the body.

Also, the article reminded me of a scene in *Chinatown*, another great movie right up there with *Casablanca*. You know the line I'm thinking about: *"No good for the glass."* I'm not going to give it away in case you haven't seen the movie, but it has to do with whether a person drowned in salt water or fresh water. At least, I think that was the clue. The movie was pretty complicated.

Regardless, the insinuation was clear in the case at hand: If there was no water in Talbot's lungs, perhaps she was murdered on the boat and then her body was dumped into the water.

"What's this got to do with anything?" hollered someone in the audience. "Are we here to solve the Talbot drowning?" asked another person.

I quickly took control of the situation.

"There were issues surrounding the death of Lilly Talbot, weren't there?" I asked Charles. Then I put the question to him in a slightly different way, "Weren't there issues surrounding the death of your third wife, Mr. Chastain?"

You could feel the jolt. It went through the audience as though everyone was seated in a pool and I had just dropped a live electrical wire in the water.

Chapter Forty-three — My Cousin Michael

"I was never accused of anything," replied Charles.

"Yet you changed your name," I replied.

"It was a big story," he said. "I was guilty in the eyes of the media. And perhaps I was guilty in the public's mind as well. At least I felt that was the case."

I could not believe it. I had him! He'd changed his name. He'd hidden his identity. He'd airbrushed his relationship with an elderly spinster whom he'd married for money, after he killed her. And still he was obfuscating at every turn.

"You hid," I thundered, "and you're still hiding now. You're equivocating every time I ask you a question. You refuse to accept reality."

I leaned in toward him. "The truth is that you went outside in the rain! You wore a raincoat you'd taken from the tavern. You went to TJK's car. When you returned, you ordered a drink for her.

"You did all of those things after killing her with an ice hook and disposing of an incriminating ice pick in the ice house in the basement of this building."

He was cool, calm and collected because he'd been in a similar situation before and gotten away with it. Twice! I couldn't allow him to walk away a third time. Could I?

I continued, "At least two times in your life, you have been involved with the death of a person who was close to you. Twelve years ago, it involved the associate dean, Gifford Winder. And, 24 years ago, the death surrounded a mysterious boating accident in which your new bride at the tender age of 84 was pulled from the Potomac River.

"You've moved past both of those cases. You even changed your name to broaden the distance between you and the past. But you can't escape the past. It's not even past, is it? It's right here in front of us tonight in the guise of TJK."

I sort of butchered that line about the past not even being the past. It's a quote from William Faulkner. The exact line is, "The past is never dead. It's not even past." The line comes from *Requiem for a Nun*. I love it because it's so true. Ten years ago, Faulkner Literary Rights LLC sought copyright infringement against Sony for the use of that language in *Midnight in Paris*. Fortunately, a court ruled the use of the quote was de minimis and constituted fair use. Based on that ruling, I feel pretty safe using it here.

Suddenly a gust of wind whipped against the windows, penetrated the building and flowed across the room. The wind was cold and moist. People shivered. The lights flickered. The building creaked, as though it was trying to speak to us. The windows shook. A last gasp of rain unleashed itself against the windows. Lightning exploded across the sky throughout Old Town.

Actually, none of those things happened. It didn't matter. I mean, it would have been a nice touch, but it wasn't necessary. Something else was happening. It was unmistakable. I was again being influenced by a spirit. This time, it was tapping into my brain.

I flashed on the part of the conversation earlier in the evening when Charles showed me Quinn's dog leash.

At that very instant, the door opened and Alexandria Deputy Police Chief Sherry Stone walked into the room. Everyone turned. She dangled something in her hand that resembled a dead snake.

Stone and Santana live together in her townhome on Prince Street, around the corner from where Katz and Abby Snowe live on Harvard Street. Stone is sort of the yin to Katz's yang, if you know what I mean. That was certainly true in the Jones Point case in 2019 as well as the mystery surrounding the explosion at Roaches Run last year.

She approached me. "We found TJK's car," she said. She removed a key fob from her pocket and held it in the palm of her hand. "It was in her purse." Ah. That told me the police were here investigating the scene of the crime. "The doors were unlocked," she continued. "The glove box was open, as was the console between the front seats. The cab had been ransacked." She handed me the "snake," which turned out to be a length of wet leather. "I found this beside the vehicle. In the gutter."

I held it up. I doubt anyone knew what it was, with the exception of Michael Charles, whose eyes welled with tears.

"This leash belonged to your dog," I addressed Charles. "You showed it to me earlier this evening. How did it end up in the gutter alongside TJK's car unless it fell out of your pocket?"

Charles stared at the leash. He blinked his eyes until the tears vanished. Then he spoke, "I don't recall bringing a dog leash with me tonight. My dog is dead." He fought back a fresh onslaught of tears. "I don't recognize it."

I could see the internal tension. On the one hand, he wanted to hold the leash. It was all he had left of Quinn, other than memories. On the other hand, if he acknowledged ownership of the leash, he would be admitting that he'd lied all along.

And, by extension, he would be implicating himself in murder.

My mind raced ahead. What had Charles been looking for inside TJK's car? Had he found whatever he'd been searching for? If so, what was it? Where was it?

The wavelength infecting my brain made me think of the ice house. Was it possible, I wondered, if something was hidden there along with the ice pick? I walked over to Santana and whispered in his ear. He turned and left the room just like Paul Drake used to do when Perry Mason (Raymond Burr) gave his PI something to track down in the middle of a trial. The courtroom dramatizations in *Perry Mason* are among the best I've ever watched, right up there with *Witness for the Prosecution* and *My Cousin Vinnie*.

Don't laugh. Joe Pesci's enactment of attorney Vinny Gambini is phenomenal, as is the questioning of Mona Lisa Vito, played by Marisa Tomei, and the cross-examination of the prosecution's witnesses. It's my understanding that portions of the film are shown in trial advocacy programs. I don't know if that's true, but it wouldn't surprise me. To avoid any allegations of copyright infringement, the story was written by Dale Launer and the movie directed by Jonathan Lynn. Tomei won an Oscar for best supporting actress for her role in the movie.

Hey, maybe they'll make a movie out of my story!

That's when I notice a dog tag hanging from the leash. Charles was staring it as well. He was probably wondering if I'd seen it. I, in turn, was hoping it identified Quinn. Imagine if it did not! If I brought attention to the dog tag and it did not identify Quinn, the case would take a giant step backwards. It was a gamble I could not afford to take.

Best to wait until Santana returned from the ice house on his errand. I texted Mai and asked her to check on him. The quicker he got back, the better.

Chapter Forty-four — The Iceman Cometh

As he later relayed to me, Curtis Santana stood in the cavernous cylindrical hole that once served as the ice house for Gadsby's Tavern.

One hundred years ago, an ice truck lumbered down the cobblestone streets of Old Town delivering blocks of ice to homes and businesses, including this ice house. When the ice house was restored, a glass ceiling was installed at street level to enable sightseers to peer down into the silo.

Because of the fierce rains and stormy blackness that shrouded Old Town this night, a person wandering in the basement would not have realized there was a skylight in the ceiling.

Santana stood in the center of the room. The overhead and wall lights were not working in the basement. Lights had flickered in the upstairs rooms earlier in the night. Perhaps a fuse had blown, Santana assumed. He took his flashlight from his pocket. Its beam was like a torch, or perhaps like a *Star Wars* lightsaber.

He turned slowly in a clockwise movement, the beam touching everything in the room. The light forced its way into hidden corners, penetrating dark shadows and crevices. In the light's beam, specks of dust danced in the air.

The room was cold and musty. Standing inside the silo felt like being in the Tower of London. Santana checked to be sure there were no chains hanging from the walls. As he moved the light around the room, he felt something grabbing his arm and directing the path of the flashlight's beam.

He lowered the beam. The light fell upon a sheaf of papers stuffed between two dusty wooden crates. There were wet footprints leading to the corner of the room where the papers had been stashed.

Santana donned a pair of latex gloves. He also moved cautiously across the floor so as not to disturb the watermarks on the cement floor. The pattern of a shoe sole was apparent. He reached over and grabbed the papers with his left hand while holding the flashlight in his right hand.

He flipped through the papers and directed the light toward them. It was an investigative report about an old case. A chill swept Santana as he realized this was the same case that David Reese had projected on the screen in the ballroom. The narrative concerned Lilly Talbot.

Suddenly, a footstep crunched down the hall. Santana looked up, dousing the flashlight.

"Curtis, are you down here?"

He recognized the voice and switched on his flashlight, landing the beam at the feet of Mai Lin. "What are you doing down here?" he asked.

"David texted me," she explained. "He wanted to me to tell you to hurry. Have you found anything?"

"Look at this," said Santana. He handed the papers to Lin and held the flashlight so that she could read the pages.

"I was just researching this case," she said excitedly as she raced through the paperwork. "This seems to have been prepared by a private investigator on behalf of an unknown client who wanted to learn the truth about what happened to Lilly Talbot." She looked at Santana. "Where did you find this, Curtis?"

He pointed to the corner where he had retrieved the papers. "Careful," he instructed. "Don't step on these footprints. I'm betting the print will match the sole of Michael Charles' shoes. And this is the area where David found the ice pick, too."

"You think Charles put both of them here?" she asked.

"You weren't in the room when David talked about the steps taken by Charles," said Santana. "David said Samantha James saw Charles return to the bar in the overcoat and then disappear for a few minutes before approaching the bar and ordering a drink for TJK.

"I think Charles retrieved these papers from TJK's car," he continued. "He had already ditched the ice pick here and he returned to the same location to store the documents. He must have believed this was a safe hiding place.

"He then returned upstairs and ordered the cosmopolitan, pretending as though she was still alive. He probably intended to come back down here at some point and retrieve both the documents and the ice pick. He intended to throw the weapon in the river and burn the documents. Pure speculation on my part, but probably close to the truth."

"This explains everything," Lin exclaimed. She clutched the papers in her hand. "TJK was blackmailing Charles with a report about the true facts and circumstances surrounding Lilly Talbot's demise. Quick, let's get upstairs and solve the murder."

They raced up the staircase and headed to the ballroom. "By the way," Santana said, spitting out words as he ran, "David's done a great job. I think he's going to put away Charles once we hand this to him."

Lin appreciated hearing those words from Santana, in whom she had confided when she'd learned of David's infidelity last year.

Working alongside U.S. Attorney Mo Katz, Lin had been exposed to the criminal underclass. She never thought of herself as naïve, but criminal court cases introduced her to a subterranean world of cheats, liars, and miscreants. As a result, she knew she could not take loyalty and honesty for granted. When David engaged in sexual liaisons outside of their marriage, she felt she had been robbed of the only safe quarter in her life.

"David's betrayal cut me to the core," she said. "It's going to take more than this for me to take him back." Yet, when they'd spoken earlier, he seemed repentant. Still, she was concerned about being lied to again *if* she did take him back. *Once fooled, shame on you. Twice fooled, shame on me.* "It'll take a special moment," she said.

They entered the meeting room.

*

Dear Reader: Some mystery readers get to a point in the story where they simply want to know one thing: Who done it? They flip to the back of the book to figure it out.

Sometimes, those readers go back and read the story in its entirety, while other times they just close the book for good.

That pisses me off. I took a lot of time to write down all of that night's proceedings, and it frosts me that anyone is neglecting my prose and just checking the box score after the game is over, so to speak.

So I'm pulling a little trick to teach them a lesson.

The next chapter is for them. I'm putting in a fake scene. I've made it easy for them to find it by using the highlighter. It may be too cute by half, but indulge me.

By the way, as you may have figured out, the highlighted sentences in this story did not all turn out to be clues. I got a little carried away with the highlighter. Sorry about that.

You can skip the next chapter and go onto the next one.

And, if you ever run into someone in Old Town who talks about this book and tells you they were surprised to read that Ash Brook was the murderer, don't correct them. They deserve to be misled.
DER

Chapter Forty-five — The Murderer Is Revealed

Ash Brook killed TJK with the champagne flute in the ice house. She had smashed the glass and then plunged its jagged edge into TJK's gullet. TJK twisted and turned like a corkscrew before falling to the ground, where she seemingly melted into a puddle like the Wicked Witch in *The Wizard of Oz*.

Throughout the evening, Ash Brook appeared to be a peripheral character in the murder mystery, someone flitting around the flame like a moth attracted to the light but who avoided the spotlight.

Until now!

The shrewd examination by David Reese, the highly esteemed Alexandria prosecutor, proved too much for her stealthy maneuvers. His techniques to uncover the truth were superior to her efforts to suppress it.

"J'accuse!" Reese yelled across the room at Ash Brook, using the line made famous by Emile Zola.

She withered under his steely examination. "It is I!" she cried. "Jealousy and rage drove me to kill her. I'm not sorry. I would do it again. And the flute proved the perfect instrument!"

Reese was applauded for his performance. A feature article of his exploits appeared on the front page of *The Washington Chronicle*. He was invited to the White House to dine with the president and first lady.

He invited Mai Lin to accompany him and, by so doing, won back her heart.

Chapter Forty-six — Three to Get Ready

Alas, if only that last sentence was true. Sometimes, if you wish hard enough for something, it actually comes true. That's why I wrote it. Fingers crossed.

As Santana and Mai returned from the ice house, I was recalling "Born This Way" and the power of that song: simple, direct, and true. Earlier, I had ceased the stop-and-go approach that resembled a four-way stop sign. Yet, as the night wore on and I'd become weary, I'd forgotten the message of "Born This Way," which might have been another reason my examination took so long to reach its fated destination.

TJK blackmailed people. I had missed that angle during my initial examinations and, even after I finally focused on it, I continued to miss the mark. However, if I was equipped with the best evidence and if I directed it at the right suspect, I knew I'd hit a bullseye.

Michael Charles was a tough nut to crack, but I was determined to bring him down.

His complicity in the crime had escaped me. There's a reason for that. It has to do with assumptions we make and the order in which things take place, or seem to take place. Sometimes we fool ourselves about what we see, or think we see, as well as the order in which things occur.

Life swirls by us and, for the most part, we don't pay attention, even when we think we're doing so. It's only when something catastrophic happens and you have to reconstruct the situation that everything loses its fluidity and becomes fixed in position.

For example, remember when I first heard the scream? I surveyed the room at that time. My assumption was that everyone in the room at that moment had been in the room at the time of the murder. Therefore, I concluded that no one in the room could have committed the crime.

Wrong.

Furthermore, at the moment I heard the scream, I thought I saw the same fear and dread in the eyes of others that I was feeling inside of myself.

Again, wrong.

My assumption that Michael Charles was innocent because he was in the room was wrong. So was my belief that his eyes conveyed the same emotion as mine. In truth, he was probably realizing that his crime had been discovered.

Suffice to say that the sequence of events — either real or perceived — can have a huge impact upon what you see, or what you think you see.

Which reminds me. All my life, I believed the Beatles' *Let It Be* album was recorded after *Abbey Road*. It turns out, however, based on the *Get Back* documentary, that *Let It Be* was recorded beforehand. That changes a lifetime of beliefs about the facts and circumstances that contributed to the dissolution of the greatest band of all time.

Why did I believe that to be the case? It was because I thought *Abbey Road* was released before *Let It Be*. See my point? A simple occurrence can lead you to believe that events unfolded in a certain way when, in fact, the reality is entirely different.

I was straightening the sequence of events out in my mind when Mai handed me the document that Curtis discovered in the ice house. And here it happened again! It was a quick handoff, like a baton in a relay race. Yet, in that instant, I felt the presence of another hand.

I've spoken to Mai about it and she confirms that she felt the same sensation. And Santana has told me that he felt something directing the angle of the flashlight when he discovered the document.

I don't want to belabor the point or claim there was some supernatural influence directing the events of that night. But I'll tell you this: I'm not going to laugh when someone says they saw the silhouette of the Female Stranger in a window at the corner of Cameron and Royal Streets.

True, there were many forces that played a role in the investigation. One was the placement of the drinking glasses. More than once, they glasses provided clues.

Another was the secrets uncovered by using the formula of McLuhan's *The Rhythmic Cycle of Life*.

But I would be lying if I suggested that the Female Stranger didn't also have something to do with it.

Now I turned back to Michael Charles. No more theatrics, I told myself. I repeated the mantra: simple, direct, true. I looked at Charles and handed the document to him.

BTW, I did not look at the document that Mai handed me. No, I didn't forget. I deliberately chose not to look at it. To do so would have demonstrated unfamiliarity with the contents. That, in turn, would demonstrate to Charles that I didn't know what was in it.

As his adroit maneuvering demonstrated over the past hour, Charles would use my unfamiliarity with the exhibit as an opportunity to weasel out of another trap.

Therefore, I decided simply to hand the papers to him and extrapolate their meaning based upon his response. Granted, there was an inherent risk, namely that his response would be an inaccurate barometer. But I'm pretty good at ad-libbing and I knew I could pull it off if I had a fighting chance.

He studied it thoroughly. "This is about Lilly Talbot," he said.

Be direct, I steeled myself. "It's about the facts and circumstances surrounding Lilly Talbot's death, isn't it?"

"It is," he replied.

I studied Charles. He looked around like a man searching for the red sign above the door that reads EXIT.

"TJK solicited the investigation, did you know that?" I asked.

"She told me she'd solicited such a report," he replied. "I'd never seen it until now."

Be truthful. "That's not exactly right, is it?" I asked. "You did see it, didn't you? You saw it when you pulled it out of TJK's car and hid it in the ice house."

No denial followed. There was no equivocation or ambiguity. Charles appeared to be running out of steam.

Be simple. "Let's cut to the chase, Mr. Charles, shall we? TJK had been bribing you for some time. Tonight, she told you she had the report with her. Armed with that information, you acted. You eliminated the threat. You killed her. And then you retrieved the evidence."

His head fell down. His chin rested on his chest. He was shaking.

Michael Charles slowly unraveled.

He shook uncontrollably for a considerable amount of time. When he spoke, the words were emitted between sobs. His eyes, nose, lips, and mouth contorted. Red spots appeared on his cheeks. His brow furrowed. His entire face turned crimson. The sobs turned into a full throttle cry. Tears streamed down his cheeks and settled in the corners of his mouth. Stuff was coming out of his nose. His tongue came out like a snake's and licked the salty tears.

He reached into his jacket breast pocket and retrieved a handkerchief. As he did so, a piece of paper floated out. It sailed through the air and right into my hand. I grabbed it the way a child would grab a falling leaf.

I read the words on the paper: "I know what you did." These were the words written by Bernie Hill after he overheard the conversation between TJK and Charles. You remember, it was the conversation he denied overhearing.

I simply held it in my hand without even bothering to read it to the audience. It was end game. There was no more room for equivocation.

"I didn't intend this," Charles said slowly. "I wasn't even supposed to be here tonight. I was supposed to be touring gardens. I never even knew there was a performance of *Murder in the Museum*. If I'd known, I doubt if I would have gone. I don't find such skits the least bit amusing or enjoyable."

Perhaps he didn't, but others found the performance extremely satisfying. Unfortunately, their enjoyment had come at his expense.

"She's the responsible party," he continued.

For an instant, I saw the defense argument, namely self-defense. The only problem, of course, was the cover-up. It's true what they say, you know. It's never the crime. It's always the cover-up. If he had simply run downstairs and immediately announced what had happened, it might have meant the difference for him between a Get Out of Jail Free card and the gallows.

But he'd gone to her car and retrieved the incriminating documentation. He'd hidden the papers and the ice pick in the ice house. He'd purchased a cosmopolitan for her after she was already dead. He could assign all the blame he wanted to TJK but it wasn't going to exonerate him. A pinprick didn't justify his action.

"Please continue," I said.

He did. Except he didn't go in the direction I expected. "Lilly was no good," he said. "She wouldn't allow me to take charge of her affairs. I only wanted to help her. I never wanted to control her. But she had to assert her independence. She had to be her own woman."

This was going to be a twofer. Who knew? In all honesty, I'd half forgotten about Lilly. It now occurred to me that a cold case was being resolved while we solved the puzzle of TJK's murder in the museum.

Michael Charles recognized that he was being recorded. He didn't seem to care. "She said she was putting all of her assets into a trust and leaving them to charity," he said. "I told her charity begins at home. She didn't seem to understand. I felt I had to bang some sense into her. I swatted her with the paddle."

He shook his head. "It was just intended as a tap. But she overreacted and fell off the boat into the water. I leaned over to render assistance, but it was evident she'd killed herself by going overboard."

What a sociopath, I thought. The next thing you know, he was going to say she'd beaten her head against the paddle.

"I tried to stop her from tumbling overboard," he continued, "but it was impossible after she bumped into the paddle."

A sheen of sweat formed over his visage. "I didn't feel bad," he continued. "I certainly wasn't responsible. Just like the associate dean."

Did I say twofer a minute ago? Correction. This was turning into a three bagger! He was now talking about the associate dean at the university, Gifford Winder.

"Go on," I said.

"He wouldn't get out of the way," said Charles. "It was time for him to retire and make room for young blood. People like me needed to advance. It was wrong of him. That's what killed him, you know, his own selfishness."

Poor Michael Charles. Perhaps we were supposed to grieve for him?

"Did you poison him?" I asked.

"He poisoned himself," Charles answered. "Nobody told him to consume that drink. Certainly not me. He's the one who raised the glass."

Listening to Charles, I realized his delay in acknowledging complicity arose from the fact that he was incapable of admitting culpability. I doubt that he's bereft of conscience. More likely, he's simply emblematic of the times in which we live. When it comes time to taking responsibility, most of us run and hide. Somewhere in the evolution of our species, a lot of us have lost our spine.

"What can you tell us about TJK?" I inquired, hiding the disgust I harbored toward him.

"She blackmailed everyone," he said. He turned to the crowd. "A lot of you were her victims. Only a few of you gave testimony today. Yet dozens of you were victims of her reign of terror. It was an epidemic, what we were dealing with because of that woman.

Someone had to provide an antidote. I ended the siege for the benefit of all of us.

"Plus," he added, "I was only defending myself. She attacked me with an ice pick. I was bleeding. She might just as easily have put a gun to my head. What choice did I have?" He stood up and faced the audience. "I did this for you as much as I did it for myself. You should all be thanking me."

Yeah, I thought to myself. We'll give you a medal. Or, rather, some metal. The door opened. The cavalry had arrived. Sherry Stone, who had been standing by listening to Charles unroll his confession, called out, "Cuff him, boys," to the officers who entered the room.

Michael Charles held out his arms. He sought to get in the last word. "I'm the victim," he said. "I didn't come here intending to be hurt by anyone. TJK viciously attacked me with her threats and with a weapon. I had no recourse."

In Charles' words, I heard the defense argument taking shape. TJK would be the one put on trial. The defense would seek to portray Charles as a sympathetic character who should be convicted of a lesser included crime and given a reduced sentence, if he should be convicted at all. And, if the defense team was really shrewd, they'd somehow finagle to get jurors on the panel who were themselves victims of TJK's machinations.

I couldn't let him end the proceeding. So I spoke up. "'Assault lies dormant within us all,'" I said. "'It requires only circumstances to set it in violent motion.'"

The audience was struck by the poignancy of those words, as I suspected they would, but I can't honestly take credit. Katherine Hepburn said those lines in the 1952 film, *Pat and Mike*, alongside Spencer Tracey.

Actually, when I think about it now, those words didn't really fit. They sound like a bit of an excuse for Charles' behavior. Yet they sounded perfect at the time.

I wondered how a jury was going to react to all of the evidence in this case. TJK was hardly a sympathetic figure. If Charles hadn't gone to such lengths to cover up his complicity, he might have been able to win favor with the jury. But his actions, combined with tonight's confession, would seal his fate, or so I assumed.

I handed over the dog leash to Stone as evidence after taking a peek at the tag. No surprise: "Quinn" was etched into the tag, along with a phone number that no doubt was Charles'.

Everyone was leaving now, and I myself found my own way to the door. Wait a second. It wasn't *Pat and Mike*. It was *Adam's Rib*, released in 1949. I always confused my Hepburn-Tracy movies. And it's Tracy, not Tracey. It must be getting late. Plus, to be honest, I'm exhausted.

Chapter Forty-seven — And in the End

People flooded onto the street looking as though they were returning from a harrowing cruise gone bad rather than a night at the theater. Perhaps *flooded* is the wrong word to use following a major storm, but it's the best I've got. Just like that movie quote. I'm pretty depleted at this point.

I found myself walking up the street with Mo Katz. He'd already congratulated me on my performance. Whatever friction existed between us earlier in the evening was gone.

"In the end, everyone has a secret," he said. "Some are embarrassing. Others are just plain funny or stupid. Nobody much cares about them, with the possible exception of the person who's the brunt of the joke. But even that person can live with it, skulking away if he's unable to shrug it off."

The streets were glazed in water. It sparkled under the street lights. Red bricks, black street tar, and cement all glistened as though they were coated with stardust. I wondered where Katz was going, both in terms of our walk and his monologue.

"Then there are the ones that matter," he continued. Katz seemed obsessed with the subject of secrets. "Those are the dangerous ones. They're dangerous because they need to remain covered up. As everyone knows, truth can't be covered up. Not forever, at least. Sooner or later, truth emerges, even if nobody notices it or cares about it any longer."

The street curved to the left. Katz walked on purposefully and I tagged along, assuming he had a destination in mind.

"Some truths expose hypocrisy," he went on. Although I walked beside him, he spoke as though he was talking to his muse. He sounded a little scatterbrained, to be honest. But I couldn't criticize him. My thoughts weren't all that coherent either. After all, we'd been up the entire night.

If you've ever pulled an all-nighter, you know the feeling. You're neither awake nor asleep, but you're certainly not in full command of your faculties. I stumbled on the pavement and hurried to catch up to Katz. I was beginning to feel as though I was Boswell to his Dr. Johnson. Or maybe I was Watson to his Holmes. It was hard to say.

"Those cases actually fall into the first category," he continued, "along with the ones that can be laughed at and excused."

Those cases? I asked myself. Which cases were *those cases?* Either I missed something or he was definitely rambling at this point.

"They're deadly because they can't be forgiven," he said. "They're mortal and punishable. They don't just sting or hurt. They kill."

Overhead, clouds separated in the sky. Patches of blue separated. The winds pushed clouds apart with a gentle ferocity. I looked up and saw stars sprinkled between puffy white bluffs.

Katz turned a corner. I quickened to keep pace.

"Where are you headed?" I asked.

"We're going to the 24-hour diner on Fayette Street," he said. "They're open, you know. The staff never left last night because of the weather. You should see the pictures they're posting on Instagram. I'm starved."

The thought occurred to me that while I had been busy investigating the murder, Katz had been going through his social media and thinking about food. Interesting. We rounded another corner. A crowd was gathered outside the door to the restaurant. I laughed. "This is so cool," I said like a little kid who was going to the local bakery to buy some sugar-glazed donuts.

We got in line, which stretched halfway down the block. It was a little eerie, to tell the truth, sort of like *Night of the Living Dead* or something. I mean, all these zombies up pre-dawn walking the streets of Old Town.

Katz stopped talking. I guess it was my turn. Actually, his words sort of resonated with me. "Is my sin mortal?" I asked in a low voice. It seemed like the kind of question more appropriate for the confessional than a food line.

"Only Mai can answer that," he said. "If you killed something inside of her, then it is. If not, then you've got a shot."

"A shot at what?"

"Redemption."

Is that how it works? I wondered. "I'm sorry for the pain I caused her," I said.

Katz shook his head as if to say, *Don't apologize to me, kid.*

"You know, it's weird about Michael Charles," I said. "I mean, I never would have suspected him of murder. And all of that stuff, you know, changing his name and everything. And dealing with the blackmail. I never suspected any of it. Did you?"

"I never met him before last night, so I can't answer that question," he said.

Of course, stupid me.

"But, as a general principle, you can't detect people's secrets," he continued. "Maybe you do sometimes, if they're really obvious. But, for the most part, secrets remain disguised. You're the only one who knows your own secrets."

Katz didn't say anything else. He wasn't even looking at me. He was just another person standing in line thinking about the food he was going to be eating in a little while.

The contours of the day suddenly started to change. It was gradual, but distinct. The buildings, the sky, the parked cars, the crowd. Everybody and everything got clearer.

Pre-dawn is a strange time. It's actually quite beautiful. The world lightens, though the sun hasn't risen. It's like someone turned on a dimmer switch.

"Hey," I said. It was a spontaneous utterance. I kind of surprised myself. "I think I'm going to go." And, with that, I stepped out of the line.

Katz noted no objection. He just shrugged and gave me a wave. He seemed preoccupied. I hardly blamed him. It had been quite a night. The *Murder in the Museum* had morphed from illusion to reality. Now it seemed we were returning to some odd illusory state of mind.

Chapter Forty-eight — The Spirits of Old Town

It took me a minute to remember where I'd parked the car. It seemed like years had passed. The car was on Strand Street, as it turned out, in that small strip of parking spaces facing the park and the water off Duke Street. You know where. It's one of those go-to places to check for parking spaces if you're trying to shop at the base of King Street.

It's about a 15-minute straight shot down King Street from the 24-hour diner. But I didn't go that way. Instead, I took the streets running perpendicular to King and cut down the alleys between them that parallel King Street, running like a ribbon of asphalt through Old Town, a grid within a grid, with names like Emerson Alley, Downham Way, and Smuggler's Alley.

I took all of them, and a few more besides. Puddles filled long stretches and I had to walk along the high edges of the asphalt or cobblestones to avoid stepping in them. Garages and the backs of restaurants and shops were to my left and right. Few lights were burning but the night was no longer dark and foreboding.

At some point, I forgot what year it was. That happens frequently when you walk the streets of Old Town. You become lost in time. I felt as though I was back in Revolutionary times or in the midst of the Civil War era. The architecture, the streets and alleys, the slope of the city toward the river all echo to the past. As so often happens, I thought I heard a horse's hoofs, a colonialist's steps, or the wheel of a carriage rolling along the street.

It's not as though ghosts appear, not exactly, but you are transported in time and you feel as though you're walking those sidewalks with them. I felt it at that moment. As though time itself was layered here, year over year, century over century, and everyone who had ever walked down this alley was here with me.

On the one hand, I was by myself. At least that's how it looked to the naked eye. Yet, to me, it felt different, as though there were hundreds of other people filling the alleys and sidewalks. An invisible crowd passing in the night, everyone on some mission in their own time. The spirits of the past, present, and future, all mixed together, everyone who ever had or ever would pass along that alley.

You might call that crazy or fanciful, but anyone who's walked through Old Town at night knows what I mean. I'm not the only person who's experienced it. It's part of the romance of this place.

No, The Female Stranger didn't make an appearance, if that's what you're waiting for me to write. If she was anywhere, it was back there at the corner of Cameron and Royal Streets.

As I approached the base of King Street, I was pulled back to reality as I witnessed the extent of the flooding. All of Strand and lower King Streets were flooded. I walked briskly toward the car, afraid I'd find it submerged and that I'd be calling the insurance company to report a total loss.

Miraculously, the parking lot had been spared a deluge. Oh, sure, it was wet, but it had only a couple of inches of water on it. Not even the tires were submerged. I hit the key fob button, the emergency lights lit, and the car beeped. As soon as I got in, the Beatles Channel began playing on the XM Sirius radio, the only channel I've been listening to since I watched *Get Back* last winter. I turned off the radio, lowered the windows, and opened the sunroof.

The engine was running and the dashboard was lit. Eventually I put the car in reverse and pulled out of the lot, turning right onto Duke Street. Then I questioned my sobriety, along with my own sanity, if I'm being completely honest.

I hadn't eaten in hours. I'd consumed several drinks, albeit hours earlier. Still, I decided not to take any chances. I found a dry space along the curb and parked. I buttoned up the car. Then I summoned an Uber.

Chapter Forty-nine — Everybody's Got Something to Hide

It took 15 minutes for a driver to pick me up. I wasn't complaining. I was glad someone was out this time of night, or morning.

The Uber driver turned onto King and drove by the Masonic Temple up Shooters Hill toward Fairlington Villages. As I sat in the back seat, morning broke. Legions of white and black clouds marched across the horizon illuminated by the first light of dawn. I opened the window. The air smelled fresh and wet.

As we crossed over I-395 and turned right into Fairlington, it occurred to me that I'd given my key to Mai. I couldn't get upstairs to knock on the door. I'd have to call and ask her to come down and open the front door.

What if she refused? I wondered. The car stopped and I got out. Tree branches and leaves cluttered the grass, sidewalk, street, and parking lot. I walked across the street and headed for the door. At the same time, a delivery car pulled up in front of our building. The driver jumped out and ran to the door. He carried a bag with the logo of the 24-hour diner where Katz and I had stood in line.

The front door opened and Mai, wearing sweats, stood there. The driver handed her the bag and she thanked him and gave him a tip. Then she glanced at me and said, "Mo said there's food for three."

Mr. Katz said that, I thought. I stepped forward, double-time. She held the door open.

As I entered the vestibule, I was acutely aware of the fact that I had damaged Mai's safe space, that place everyone needs to feel secure. *Gimme Shelter.* No one has the right to violate someone else's safe space, but that's what I'd done. And it was terrible thing.

But if Mo Katz was right, it was only fatal if Mai did not forgive me.

She handed the bag to me. The food smelled delicious. "Let's go upstairs before the moment passes," she said.

"Listen," I said. "I have something to tell you." I was embarrassed, but the source of my embarrassment, as you are about to learn, was also the source of my salvation. "I did go out with Patricia," I said, "but it's not what you think." I took a deep breath and blurted it out. "I couldn't perform."

There it is. I'm sharing my secret. I never had sex with Patricia Blu. Yes, we went to a hotel. The problem was, I couldn't start a fire under the sheets. I'm super embarrassed to share something so personal with you. But I had to tell Mai and, well, you're along for the ride. Except, please, don't tell anyone else.

"I know," she smiled. "Patricia told me."

"She told you?" I replied, stunned.

"Yes," answered Mai. "I was in her shop the other week. She shared everything with me. She said it was her idea, that she basically seduced you. According to her, you froze up when the moment of truth arrived. You're not a player, David. Maybe in your imagination, but not in real life."

It's true. When push came to shove that night — so to speak — I felt conflicted. I love Mai, you see. I couldn't get her out of my mind, even though I was in the arms of another woman. And I couldn't reconcile my actions. Except, of course, on that one prior occasion.

"So you forgive me?" I asked contritely.

"Not entirely," she said.

I was about to make a complete confession when she added: "I know about that one, too."

I started to cry.

"You're a good guy but you're still an idiot, David," she said. "I will never forgive you entirely. But I'm not going to discard you. You have your admirable qualities. And, most importantly, I love you."

"I love you, too," I said. "And I am sorry. Very, very sorry." We kissed. Then we climbed the steps to our apartment. Light shone through the small octagon window on the landing between the 2nd and 3rd floor, lighting the stairwell.

The next morning was glorious. We stayed in bed. Our son joined us at some point and we tossed around together. We made tents, igloos, and caves out of the blankets. Then we created a mess of the kitchen making pancakes. Afterwards, we went outside. The blue sky was punctuated by the brilliance of the sun. Not a cloud swept across the sky. We walked to a park and sat in swings while our son played on the climbing equipment.

"I wonder what'll happen to Michael Charles?" I asked.

"He'll go to trial and will end up being convicted of first degree for TJK's murder," said Mai. "Then they'll indict him for the other two murders."

As always, she was spot-on.

Here's what happened six months later:

Charles' attorneys filed motions to suppress his confession. They claimed that, although he was never formally in police custody, he had been interrogated by a state prosecutor and his freedom to terminate the interview was hampered by the presence of police officers in the building.

These arguments proved unpersuasive and the motions were denied.

Having exhausted every conceivable motion to suppress the confession, Charles still went to trial. He testified. Didn't I tell you that's the "in" thing to do these days?

He admitted he had killed TJK. But, his defense team argued....

....He should be convicted of a lesser included crime because he had not formed the requisite intent prior to the moment when he thrust the ice hook into her.

...He had acted in the heat of passion in response to her threats to blackmail him.

...He should be acquitted because she struck him with an ice pick and therefore he acted in self-defense.

The jury didn't buy anything he and his attorneys were selling.

The verdict was guilty in the first degree. The foreperson who delivered it was a woman who dressed throughout the trial in colonial garb. Nobody had seen her before she appeared for jury duty and no one has seen her since the jury returned its verdict.

Out of curiosity, I looked up her residence after the case was concluded. According to the courthouse records, she resides on Hamilton Road. I have no doubt she was the same person who guided me to the ice house on the corner of Cameron and Royal Streets and who got inside my head during the final leg of my questioning of Michael Charles.

Her name was Theodosia Florence Sunn. T.F.S.

According to statements by other jurors, she was a very persuasive member of the panel and steered the discussion away from the self-defense argument and toward the finding of guilt.

Strange, but true.

Later, at the sentencing hearing, which took place a few weeks after the jury returned its verdict, Charles' attorneys acknowledged the jury's verdict. But, they argued...

...TJK was a despicable monster who had bribed Charles for years. Therefore, leniency was appropriate because Charles had suffered unduly at her hand.

...A suspended sentence was appropriate because it was his first murder and she deserved to die anyway.

None of those arguments proved persuasive. The judge imposed a life sentence.

Chapter Fifty — Home Sweet Home

Marital bliss is a wonderful thing. I write that as I am securely ensconced in my home again. We even bought a dog, a Golden Retriever. His name is Johnnie Blaze. It's J.B. for short, but I don't like using the initials because people assume the dog's name is James Bond.

I have returned to my duties as an assistant commonwealth attorney with renewed vigor. People approach me and say that I should challenge the incumbent commonwealth attorney in the next election. I have no desire to do so. I've never been a political person and I'm not going to start now. I'm perfectly content to be a lawyer.

If Mo Katz leaves the U.S. Attorney's Office, I'd jump at the chance to join him in private practice. Katz & Reese, Attorneys at Law, has a certain ring to it. If not, I'll stay where I am. Either way, I'm waiting for a new case to come at me with lightning speed when I'm least expecting it.

If you're in Old Town, drop by the Commonwealth Attorney's Office in the courthouse to say hello. I'd love to meet you. Maybe we can grab a cup of coffee over at Misha's or something.

Do take care of yourself.

Oh, by the way, we're planning to have that *Murder in the Museum* thing again sometime later this year. I hope you get a chance to attend. We're going to take every imaginable precaution to prevent a repeat of what happened the first time around. But you never know, do you?

ACKNOWLEDGEMENTS

Thank you for supporting my Old Town mystery series. *Gadsby's Corner* is a work of fiction. The configuration of rooms, the items inside of those rooms, and the passages and staircases between the buildings are fictional. If you are familiar with the museum and the restaurant, you know that my portrayal does not comport with reality.

Please don't go to the Alexandria Commonwealth Attorney's Office and ask to speak to David Reese about your parking ticket. The receptionist won't know who you're talking about unless, of course, he or she has read the book. All of my characters are the product of my imagination.

Gadsby's Corner is intended to take a little slice of Old Town and turn it into a fun read.

My gratitude to Peter Arzberger, Gigi and John Flynn, Tim Harazin, Leslie Weber Hoffman, Lisa Horowitz, Dov Lutzker, Donna McDaniel, Mary Oleck, Ruth Hersh Perry, Joy Salpini, Gordon and Barbara Scott and their wonder dog Sunny, Todd and Sharon Voeltz, and Elisa Voigt for their comments and edits and for their continued friendship, support, and inspiration. Gigi is the author of a fabulous children's book, *The Imaginary Castle*.

Several devoted book club members have enthusiastically supported my series over the past years and I am grateful to each of them, including Nicole Bransome, Dana Daspit, Susie Davis, Marlene Ghormley, Lori Crow Howard, Caroline Klam, Rachel Messman, Diane Mullens, Lib Mueller, Jill Sidford, Anne Simon, Anne Smith, Maggie Tomasello, Emily Wilkinson, and Willie Wright.

Meg Power, Linda Ely and Jim Crouch, David O. Banks, Bill Finerfrock, Barry Meuse, and Kathy and John Russell are dear friends who have also provided me support and encouragement since the inception of the series.

I thank Alex White for her incredible editing and proofreading and, of course, my editors, Charles Rammelkamp and Robin Herron, for catching my errors and applying brakes to my literary excesses. If any typos remain, blame me! I put them there in the first place.

I am indebted and grateful to Gadsby's Tavern Museum Society, which helped plan the "Murder in the Museum" event that was the genesis of this book. In particular, I thank Sue Johnson and Liz Williams, who reviewed the manuscript and offered helpful suggestions.

I also thank Beth Lawton and Mary Ann Barton at *Alexandria Living Magazine*; Ralph Peluso and Mary Waldron at *The Zebra Press*; Ellen Klein at Hooray for Books; Bernard Reaves at Harambee Books & Artwork, where I debuted Book Three in the series; Valerie Ianieri at The Old Town Shop; Melanie Fallon and the staff at the Alexandria Visitors Center located on King Street, where my series is displayed; Don Alexander and Rachel Baker at The Company of Books in Del Ray; and booksellers and managers at Barnes & Noble bookstores throughout Northern Virginia and the Maryland suburbs, as well as the B&N store located near the campus of Catholic University.

I would be remiss if I didn't thank other bookstores and venues, near and far, that have consistently welcomed me, including Busboys & Poets in the District, the Poe Museum in Richmond, Book Warehouse in Williamsburg, The Winchester Book Gallery, One More Page Books in Arlington, and the military Exchange stores at Fort Belvoir in Fairfax County and Fort Myer in Arlington County.

Now to the person I wish to thank most of all. With appreciation, admiration and love, this book is dedicated to Clarinda Harriss.

The Old Town mystery series featuring U.S. Attorney Mo Katz would not exist without her.

In 2015, Clarinda, publisher and editor of Baltimore's BrickHouse Books, rejected the manuscript for *Daingerfield Island*, the first book in the series. I received a detailed account of everything that was wrong with the story. I didn't tear up the rejection. I found myself agreeing with most of its points. I rewrote the story from scratch, paying strict attention to the suggestions that were included in her letter.

After I resubmitted the manuscript. I got a phone call to drive to Baltimore to meet with her and Charles Rammelkamp. In 2017, Clarinda published *Daingerfield Island*. Charles became my editor. And Clarinda introduced me to readers who would play an important role in the development of Mo and his entourage.

Equally important, Clarinda provided me with confidence. She was like the Wizard of Oz who had a diploma to award for smarts, a clock to remind me of a beating heart, and a medal for courage. In a word, she *believed* in me. She always supported the next chapter in the Mo Katz saga.

Clarinda is a literary legend in Baltimore. She served for years as a teacher at Towson University. And she is the author of several books. To me, she was more than a teacher, publisher, and fellow author. She's my friend.

Every time we got bogged down in some minutia in the process of publishing one of my books, Clarinda had a word of encouragement: "Onward!" It was a mantra for me and for countless other students, writers and artists. That word will always be in my mind when I think about everything she did to advance my work. "Onward!" indeed.

Unfortunately, Clarinda will be moving on and BrickHouse Books will be closing its doors. Thus, I have started my own enterprise, Alendron Publishing LLC, and *Gadsby's Corner* is its first book. I'll be bringing the Old Town Mystery Series featuring Mo Katz to my new company over time. And I'm going to be scouting for local talent to add to the Alendron portfolio.

BUY OLD TOWN MYSTERIES

To order paperbacks online, I recommend MADE IN ALX (www.madeinalx.com) or Itasca Books Distribution & Fulfillment (https://itascabooks.com). Paperback, ebook, and audiobook editions are also available at Amazon.com, Apple Books, Audible, Barnes and Noble, Google, Libro.fm, and Kobo. If you're in Old Town Alexandria, the paperbacks are available at the Made in Alexandria store located at 533 Montgomery Street. If I'm around, let me sign it for you! Thanks.

Daingerfield Island. The inaugural Old Town mystery opens with the discovery of a body floating in the Potomac River off Daingerfield Island, south of Reagan National Airport. Mo Katz unlocks the mystery behind the drowning based upon a photo in a locket worn around the deceased woman's neck.

Jones Point. An attorney's mysterious murder and a plot to smuggle surface-to-air missiles into Washington, D.C., culminate in a firefight on the Wilson Bridge spanning the Potomac River. Book Two of the series introduces Alexandria policewoman Sherry Stone as a newest member of the Old Town mystery crew.

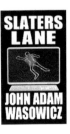

Slaters Lane. A senior prosecutor is brutally assaulted on Easter Sunday, setting off an investigation during the early stages of the COVID-19 pandemic. A complex mother-daughter relationship adds to the intrigue surrounding the assault.

 **Roaches Run.** A new age guru's theory about a 12-year cycle of life offers insight into a clash between individuals seeking retribution for past transgressions. An explosion at the Roaches Run waterfowl sanctuary outside Washington, D.C., results in an unsavory character reaping one's just deserts.

The Old Town mystery series will return in *Wilkes Tunnel*.